Never Too Late

Charming and inspiring short stories,
written especially for seniors

Ruth Philbrick

First published by Busybird Publishing 2015
Copyright © 2015 Ruth Philbrick

ISBN 978-1-925260-73-1

This is a work of fiction. Any similarities between places and characters are a coincidence.

Cover image: Ruth Philbrick
Internal Illustrations: Ruth Philbrick
Cover design: Busybird Publishing
Layout and typesetting: Busybird Publishing
Editor: Melissa Cleeman

Busybird Publishing
PO Box 855
Eltham Victoria
Australia 3095
www.busybird.com.au

To my beloved husband and best friend

Robin,

who first encouraged me to share my stories.

Contents

Acknowledgements

Firstly, thank you to my understanding editor, Melissa Cleeman, who patiently journeyed with me every step of the way.

Thanks also to the rest of the team at Busybird Publishing, and Blaise van Hecke in particular, who produced this book in a friendly, helpful manner.

And I'm grateful for the many others who surround me with love, support, and encouragement …

For my adult 'children'– Murray, Stephanie, and Catherine; all writers of excellence, each with an inspiring story to tell.

For my extended family, so many of whom have faced tragedy with true courage.

This also applies to some of my dear friends.

You all enrich my life, and I treasure you.

Preface

I hope you enjoy reading short stories as much as I do – especially those with a little surprise here or there.

I hope you'll enjoy these stories, too.

They remind us that it's NEVER TOO LATE to ...

- do something worthwhile for others
- contribute time and expertise
- develop new friendships, or nurture existing ones
- simply brighten another's day
- enjoy fellowship within a community group setting
- discover love
- act upon new opportunities
- enjoy being alive!

No, it's NEVER TOO LATE to find fulfilment and joy in the autumn years.

R.P.

Never Too Late

Susan scurried around her new little home, tidying and straightening whenever she noticed something that could be improved in a matter of seconds. She checked the clock with increasing panic as the minutes flew by. Tom would ring the doorbell at any moment. She knew he would not be late.

I'm glad I managed to set the table before I left for work this morning, she thought. He could sit there with a drink and watch the television news while she fiddled in the kitchen. The corn chowder soup was ready, but the delicate veal entrée would have to be watched.

It had been quite a feat to be ready by six o'clock. Susan worked all day, but was actually semi-retired, and looked forward to full retirement soon. She'd recently asked two of her daughters to take over management of her catering service, and they happily agreed. She could then have more time to herself, but for now, Susan still enjoyed the interaction with valued staff and clients.

Married at nineteen, and with four children born in rapid succession, Susan hadn't counted upon being a widow by the age of twenty-six! Her business had started at home, out of sheer necessity. She could then be with her children, while learning to compete in the food industry. When her youngest child started school, she moved the business out of home. It was a success, but she'd never made a fortune from it.

The sound of a car door brought her thoughts back to the present moment. She was glad she'd made sure she'd be alone with the new man in her life. She smiled at the thought. New? Well, not really, but no one else had known about her deep feelings for Tom. Their friendship had developed while she was still at school.

The doorbell rang. Susan hastily removed her apron and smoothed her new dress. She could see his tall, lean frame through the textured glass panel at the side of the door. She noted with surprise the feeling of excitement she felt, just knowing he was there. Snatching a quick glance in the hallway mirror, she made certain that her face was wearing a smile, rather than a look that might reveal anxiety. What if he'd changed his mind in the two days since they were last together?

She opened the door with seeming confidence, but didn't have a chance to read the expression on his face as he stepped inside. In a matter of seconds, she was securely in his arms, being kissed with great enthusiasm and warmth. It felt wonderful! Just as she'd imagined it would be, way back when she was seventeen.

Why should she be surprised? This was the friend she'd treasured so dearly back then. She knew that her loving feelings towards him were genuinely reciprocated, but Tom had held back on expressing them romantically. He said that their eleven-year age gap was just too great. He knew that gossip-mongers would have a field day if they knew. There seemed to be no choice but to go their separate ways (although they still privately hoped for a future together some day).

Still standing quietly in the hallway, neither wanting to let go, Susan contentedly remained in Tom's arms, not a word needing to be said. Her thoughts continued, recalling the difficult decision that had separated them.

Distraught, Susan tried to forget Tom. Two years later she was encouraged by her parents to marry her ex-classmate, Bobby. She would always be thankful that her husband had done his best to take care of them all, and she'd tried hard to be a good wife and mother, but deep down, she'd wondered about their long-term future. There was no doubting their youthful love, but they had no shared interests apart from their children, and with four of them, money was always a problem. Their marriage wasn't a strong one.

And so it was that when Bobby was killed in a hit-and-run accident, Susan closed that chapter of her life with great sadness. With the tragic loss of her husband and beloved father of her children, she now faced huge responsibilities. Despite the exhausting demands of single parenting, she found that she enjoyed making her own way in the world and was surprised to find that she liked her independence.

Susan looked up at Tom, and smiled. She'd always liked his confident, manly demeanour. For how long had they been standing there, just holding each other and savouring the closeness? She decided it didn't matter. What a nice feeling that was, to know that she was under no time pressure at all. She broke the silence first.

'Wow! You certainly know how to get the evening off to a good start. Welcome to my home,' she said happily, fanning her round face with her hand.

Tom grinned broadly and, with mock formality, bowed his head and nodded.

'Thank you, Susie, and may I say, you're looking very pretty tonight,' he said, using his old name for her. He stood back at arm's length, taking in her loveliness.

'Well, I will admit that I've tried to look my best for you,' Susan said, blushing. 'But I bet you wouldn't want to see me first thing in the morning, with my hair tangled and no makeup!'

Gently rebuking, Tom replied, 'Now that's where you're wrong, young lady. Before too long, I hope I'll get to see you any hour of the day or night.'

'Well, don't say you haven't been told,' she warned light-heartedly.

Tom chuckled as he gently closed Susan's front door.

She ushered him across the lounge room to the dining table, with its bowl of camellias that she'd so carefully arranged earlier. Tom poured two drinks, which they enjoyed while focusing on each other for a few minutes. She then excused herself, turned on the television, and tiptoed into the bedroom for a quick check in the full-length mirror.

Her golden brown hair was in a new short style, which suited her well. Her aquamarine dress flattered both her curvy figure, and her blue-green eyes. She re-applied her lipstick; a task that she hadn't expected would be necessary so early in the evening! She smiled. She was more than happy with cuddles and kisses, but that would be all. Tom had always been a gentleman, treating Susan like the young lady she was.

Susan moved to the kitchen to stir the chowder and adjust the entrée's oven temperature. She then returned to the dining nook with some warm dinner rolls. From a nearby drawer, Susan produced a small maroon gift box with a birthday card attached. She brought it over to Tom, placing it next to his serviette. She planted a little kiss on his cheek, then seated herself opposite so she could watch his reaction as he opened it.

'It's for you, my darlin', with all my love. See? I've remembered your birthday, even though it's been a while.'

Tom thanked her, then began to search through all of his jacket and trouser pockets, brows knitted with fake concern. When he found what he was looking for, his frown turned into a mischievous grin, as he overtly transferred a tiny pink satin gift bag from a back pocket into the front of his jacket.

'And I haven't forgotten yours either, sweetheart. It's easy to remember when they're a day apart, isn't it? Every birthday, I've wondered if maybe this would be the year for making contact again. I didn't know your surname when you married, so I couldn't get in touch. And suddenly, here we are, talking about our *own* marriage. I can't believe our paths finally crossed after seeing you at the greengrocer's!'

'And I was too scared to contact you, in case you'd settled down with someone else,' Susan added.

Tom realised he'd been mindlessly tinkering with the cutlery in anticipation of what he was about to say next. He stopped, looked at Susan steadily, and enclosed her small hand in both of his, the gifts ignored for a moment.

'I haven't asked you this before and you don't have to answer. But I'd like to know ... It's a question that still bothers me. Why did you give up on me? I know I called things off with our friendship, but I was prepared to wait until you were a bit older – however long it took for your parents to accept me. I know the timing wasn't perfect with you being so young, but I'm sure that you loved me every bit as much as I loved you. Was it all about the age difference?'

'Yes, it was, darlin',' Susan nodded slowly. 'I was afraid to tell my parents about us. I knew they'd disapprove – you knew too. And neither of us liked keeping our friendship a secret. It made it seem as though we were doing something shameful. The problem was my age, and nothing else.' Susan lowered her voice and her eyes as well, as she tried to explain further. 'I suppose I was angry at you when we stopped seeing each other, even though you'd explained it was the right thing to do at the time. So I married Bobby when another chance of happiness came along.'

Tom's kind, expressive face showed he was trying to understand.

Susan continued, her voice full of emotion.

'Believe me, Tom, I've regretted hurting you ever since. I thought you were wonderful. You were the kindest, most interesting person I'd ever met. I broke my own heart as well as yours. But by the time I came to my senses, I'd married someone else. That wasn't fair on Bobby, but I did love him, and I have a beautiful big family to remember him by.' Susan appeared troubled by her recollections, as two tiny tears trickled down her cheeks.

Tom reached across the table to gently dab them with his spare handkerchief.

'So … do you have any doubts about marrying me now?' he asked, his deep voice faltering a little.

'Not one,' Susan replied, her glistening eyes looking straight into those of the man she still loved.

Tom gave a big sigh, his face showing a mixture of relief and joy.

'That's what I needed to hear, sweetheart. The reason I've stayed single is because of you. Honestly, I've never really loved anyone but you, Susie. I'd like to marry you soon, if you'll agree.'

'I'd like that very much,' she responded. 'And yes, I do agree. As far as I'm concerned, the sooner the better. We're old enough to know our own minds. I've talked to my children about your proposal. I'm sure they'll come around once they've had time to think about it. They know I love you and think the world of you, and they can see how happy I am.' Her eyes twinkled. 'And they know that we can't be marrying for money, because neither of us have very much at all, more's the pity!' she teased.

They both laughed, as the slow background music coaxed them out of their seats to sway and dance. Then it was back to the dining alcove for a rest. They realised they had a little less stamina than originally thought!

Tom finally withdrew the hidden pink satin gift bag from his pocket and presented it to Susan with a tender little speech. Both opened their birthday presents with the eagerness of children and with even greater delight, as they discovered their contents. Susan's gift to Tom was an antique watch, with "For all our tomorrows" engraved on the back, while Tom's for Susan was a lovely aquamarine and diamond engagement ring, with their names inscribed on the inside of the band.

'Oh, Tom! It's beautif–' Susan stopped and sniffed the air. 'The entrée!' she declared. 'It'll be burnt!'

An ear-piercing smoke alarm beeped, as the cook dashed across to the smoky kitchen in a futile effort to rescue the blackened veal.

Tom's eyes widened in panic, as he hastily pulled his hearing aid from his ear. To his annoyance, it dropped to the floor, getting lost in the carpet. He decided to leave it there for a moment, so he could lend Susan a hand.

Susan opened the kitchen stepladder in order to use it herself, but Tom gallantly took over. He climbed up the little ladder and steadied himself. Susan wrapped her arms around his waist in case he lost his balance. Tom reached up and pressed the button on the noisy device, which stopped the alarm.

'I can see through you, Susie!' he teased, her arms still wrapped around him. 'Any excuse for a hug!'

Giggling, she turned on the exhaust fan and took the dismal remains of the entrée outside to the bin. They both admitted they were quite hungry, as the romantic evening's important conversation and exchange of gifts, (along with the food disaster) had taken its toll.

However, just as Susan put the charred ovenware in the sink to soak and had started to reheat the chowder, the doorbell rang. She wisely turned the soup off again to avoid another disaster. Exasperated at another interruption, Susan took her time walking to the door to answer.

Tom was now under the dining table on hands and knees, carefully searching for his dropped hearing aid.

Susan opened the front door only a little, when a tribe of partygoers, young and old, barged through, all bellowing, 'SURPRISE!' With animated voices and lots of laughter, they marched across into the middle of the lounge room.

Tom crawled out from under the dining table, completely baffled, but glad to have his hearing aid in place again. He rubbed his knees and sat on the comfy dining chair again. Then, inexplicably, another high-pitched, deafening smoke alarm beeped, but this time, above where everybody had gathered in the lounge room. With a pained expression, and a sigh of exasperation, Tom removed his hearing device again. He hoped one of the visitors would climb the ladder this time!

'Tom! It's my family!' yelled Susan above the din. Then the excited group parted, to reveal an amazing source of light, heat and smoke. Positioned side by side on a sturdy coffee table, and smuggled in by Susan's great-grandchildren, were two large decorated birthday cakes.

One cake, with the word 'Susan', was aglow with seventy-eight candles, while Tom's cake was ablaze with a magnificent eighty-nine!

Ray of Sunshine

Whenever Raymonda introduces herself to someone new, she always uses the same words: 'I'm Ray of Sunshine. Yes, Ray's my name and I've lived in Sunshine all my life. Lovely to meet you.' She explains this offering her hand and a cheeky smile.

'Ray of Sunshine' is certainly apt, due to her warm, bright, outgoing personality. Sunshine is the name of her home suburb. It's also the location of a nursing home here in Evergreen Road, where I work and Ray volunteers.

My own name's Cassie. I've come to appreciate just how much Ray contributes towards creating a friendly atmosphere around here. Ever reliable, on Mondays, Wednesdays and Fridays, she fronts up to the workstation counter and asks me for the name of anyone who's been a bit down, or hasn't had a visitor for a while. Then I leave her to work her magic.

I leave her to work her magic.

Her knock on the doors of the various rooms is almost always welcomed.

Ray has a small mellow-toned musical keyboard that she plays by ear, as long as she's heard the song before – and she knows them all! She's not a trained music therapist but she plays well, and has instinctive people skills. She asks for the favourite songs of those she visits, leading them through a winding road of reminiscence. She sings a little, too, and encourages each resident to join in. Together, they sing, sometimes giggle, or occasionally even shed a tear as the music brings past memories bubbling to the surface.

Ray doesn't shy away from visiting the more challenging residents in high care, either. Even those who no longer speak sometimes show a glimmer of recognition in their eyes, as she plays or sings a song that might awaken something vaguely familiar from years gone by. Ray's ability to listen patiently to personal stories is a real gift and never a chore for her.

'The people here are all lovely, Cassie,' she tells me. 'Even if one or two are having a bit of a grumpy day. I know there's always a reason for being out of sorts. Some are real scamps, aren't they? They make me laugh and then they laugh along with me. Goodness me! Is that the time already?' she says, checking her watch.

I often need to remind her if a resident has

to prepare for the next meal or activity. Ray enjoys her sessions so much that she often goes overtime. If I thank her for her wonderful work, she says quietly, 'I'm the one who should be thanking all of you! I love every moment.'

One day, Ray approached me at the work station. We got onto the topic of the popular *Little Golden Books* that had been her favourites as a young child, as well as mine.

'The children in the family are bit too old for them now,' she said, shaking her head. Her face suddenly lit up. 'What about here, Cassie? I could try reading them to a couple of people with more advanced dementia, like Jean and Ruby.'

'I'm not sure that'll work, Ray,' I replied. 'Those ladies don't show any interest in the magazines we show them.'

'It's just a little experiment, Cassie. Now and then they respond to the rhythm of music, so why not try a bit of rhyming verse? And the pictures might help too,' she suggested, hopefully.

I remembered my own parents reading those books to my brothers and me. We'd loved the illustrations and memorised the words, as had my own children. They'd enjoyed the repetition, as littlies always do. Some of the people in high care still live in their childhood. They want to dress up or cuddle soft toys or dolls. I finally agreed that the books might be worth a try and gave Ray the go-ahead.

The next afternoon, in the high care day room, I joined in with those who were occupied with activities. With help from carers and the activities team, some of the residents played snakes and ladders, wove their own place mats, or placed colourful shiny stickers onto wall hangings, each according to their capabilities. Others were exercising together in a group, or just dozing.

On time as usual, Ray appeared in the doorway with a tote bag containing her treasured little books and came over to ask if she could get started.

'I think the three of us could sit over there, Cassie,' she said, pointing to a quieter, vacant spot in one corner.

'Good idea,' I agreed, and left to escort Jean and then Ruby over to the nook. Ray fossicked in her bag while I seated the ladies in some comfortable armchairs. Then I stepped back to silently observe, perching on a nearby cube-shaped cushion.

Holding out the first book so the ladies could see the pictures, Ray started her reading slowly, while establishing eye contact. Her cheery face became more and more animated, as she tried to keep her listeners engaged, exaggerating the expression, playing around brilliantly with the characters' voices, and making funny, squishy faces, until the book was finished. I laughed at each and every one.

'Should I keep going, Cassie?' she called across to me. I didn't have to answer.

'Yes!' yelled quite a few of the residents nearby, echoed by others from further down the room.

'More!' shouted carers, helpers and some curious visitors.

Realising that she now had a wider audience for the next book, but still focusing on her two ladies, Ray rummaged through her tote bag again. She fished out a bright blue shaggy wig and popped it on her head. Next, she passed some pink ones to Jean and Ruby, who immediately cuddled and stroked them.

Ray began to read book number two. Halfway through the story, Ruby's lips became mobile, as she tried to frame some words during a repetitive rhyme. I couldn't believe it! Soon after, Jean reached over to pat some colourful illustrations – perhaps familiar ones from childhood. It warmed my heart to see them respond to Ray's idea so quickly.

With each turn of the page, Ray projected her voice a little further. As her antics and funny rubbery faces became more and more outlandish, she could see that people from all around the room were turned towards her, wanting to join in, myself included.

'Come on, everyone! Can you help me tell the story?' she called.

'Yes!' we replied enthusiastically, anticipating some merriment.

Clapping, stamping and waving our arms, staff and residents together tried to mimic her zany actions and rubbery faces, throwing in a few of our own. We, along with some of those in our care, called out any familiar words that we could recall from long ago, especially during the recurring rhymes.

Ray poked out her tongue quite a bit. So did we, but Jean's and Ruby's tongues were working overtime! People in the day room were glowing with pleasure as story time came to an end, with hearty applause for Ray. The dayroom had come alive!

Perhaps all that clowning around, especially from professional staff, was not in line with the image that nursing home management tries to project to the public. You know what I mean – that we always treat the people in our care with dignity and respect. And, of course, we do. But everyone needs times of pure innocent fun, and our shining Ray provided us all with just that.

Ray taught me a lot that day. She's forever coming up with creative ideas. I now encourage new volunteers to watch how she interacts with the residents, tailoring her conversation or activity to each person's needs or abilities.

She's wonderful. I know of the mountains she's had to climb in order to become the person I admire so much today. Only the senior staff members know of Ray's own deeply tragic story. That's the way she wants it, and we respect her wishes.

***

Oh, dear! My report writing will have to wait. It's nearly five o'clock already!

I look up from my desk to see Ray approaching. Despite her big smile, she looks tired from the afternoon's visiting.

'Would you like to eat dinner in your room, tonight, Ray?' I ask her. 'You look as though you could use an early night.'

Looking relieved, she nods in agreement and whispers thanks. I collect her pain medication, grip the handles of her wheelchair, and take her to her cosy room just down the hallway. I make sure that she manages to swallow each tablet, then go through the familiar routine of preparing her for bed. She asks for just a cuppa and a sandwich, but nods off before I've finished tucking her in.

God bless you, little Ray of Sunshine. You deserve a really good night's sleep and the sweetest of dreams.

The Pianola

The Reverend Kevin Lawrence woke to the sound of his own snoring. He'd dozed off once again during his favourite detective show on television. An afternoon rest was one of his retirement treats, with the habit established over the past fourteen years or so. He no longer felt guilty about it, and secretly felt that the indulgence was well-earned and much needed.

With some effort, due to his arthritic knees, he rose from his comfy chair, stretched and shuffled toward his family's old heirloom. Although it had the appearance of a piano, it was actually a pianola. Just about anyone could play it!

Kevin opened the lid that covered the keyboard, wiping the well-worn ebony and ivory keys with a small cloth. He'd been keeping the brass trim and timber cabinet polished, just as his wife had done. He'd buffed the mahogany finish to an impressive lustre and oiled the squeaky pedals. Once, he'd even unfurled the punched paper rolls, so that he could repair the little splits that came with wear and tear. Now, even the repairs needed further repair!

However, there was one thing that Kevin hadn't been able to bring himself to do. Although he'd often played the instrument in the past, he hadn't done so since Margaret had died.

Kevin decided that three years was long enough. Today was going to be the day.

In anticipation, he flexed his hands and rubbed them together as he used to do when pretending he was a brilliant pianist. He then adjusted his spectacles and smoothed his white moustache.

'Well, here goes, Margie,' he whispered.

Although he believed she was in a better place, he sometimes found himself talking to her, nonetheless.

Kevin chose her favourite pianola roll and placed it into its cavity. Seated comfortably at the keyboard, he adjusted the tempo lever and started the steady pedalling, filling the hidden bellows. Air was forced through the tiny paper perforations, as the roll moved slowly downwards, where it was taken up on a lower spool. This produced not only the familiar piano music, but also caused the keys to skip up and down, as though being played by an invisible pianist!

He cleared his throat and started to sing Margie's song. Kevin's was never a solo voice – more suited to being in a choir. It had been tuneful and could produce volume if needed, but Margie had been able to sing any solo piece perfectly. Her tone was sweet and pure. Her top notes clear, with not a trace of shrillness, her lower notes warm and mellow. She could have performed at large concerts, but her aim was to connect with people on a more intimate level. She liked to chat with her listeners afterwards, so preferred smaller gatherings. With true humility, she used her gift to inspire, to tell a story, to bring comfort, or just to spread a little sunshine.

Kevin started to sing, 'When you come to the end of a perfect day,' but, becoming very breathless and slightly emotional, he could hardly get to the end of the first verse. It also didn't help that his arthritic knees were also calling for him to stop pedalling. They must have deteriorated more than he'd realised over the years.

There was a decision to be made. What was the use of a pianola that wasn't being used? He wanted to pass it on to someone in his family. He asked each of his children who, in turn, spoke with their partners and children.

'I'll be honest with you, Dad,' Clive said, 'it just wouldn't blend with our contemporary décor.'

Well, that was no surprise, Kevin thought.

Russell said, 'Dad, our boys are all into electronic music now. They remember nice times when they were kids, but I think they see themselves as a bit too cool for a pianola these days.'

I think I know who sees himself as too cool, mused Kevin. *And it's not his boys!*

Wesley had at least given it some serious thought.

'Dad, we all had lots of good times around the pianola, but I think you mightn't have noticed it's in need of a bit of restoration. Some of its parts need to be repaired or replaced. The tuning needs fixing, as well. A technician for all that would charge thousands of dollars!'

Sarah was Kevin's last hope.

'I'm terribly sorry, Dad,' she said. 'All the family love it – we really do. There's just no way it will fit into our small rooms. Our furniture makes it a tight squeeze as it is.'

Kevin tried to hide his disappointment. He'd thought that Sarah would use and value the pianola more than anyone else.

'Don't feel too badly, Sarah. Everything has a use-by date, so I guess I've just got to face the music, so to speak. It's time to say goodbye to the pianola.'

Kevin had finally conceded.

***

Kevin's home was across the road from St. Mark's Church, which he'd been attending since retirement. His last appointment, the Church in which he'd completed his ministry, had been in a suburb close to the city. The strict ruling was that all retired clergy should worship in a different area and become part of that congregation. So Kevin and Margaret moved away from the vicarage and bought a small house in a newer outer suburb. It was the first home they'd ever owned.

Some happy years were spent there, as they met new friends through the parish weekday community programs, a prayer group, and Sunday services. Together, the couple enjoyed not only those activities, but the home hospitality that had been a feature of their marriage until Margaret's passing. Afterwards, Kevin asked for time to be alone and his friends gave him the space he needed. Privately working through his grief, he eventually returned to the Sunday services, but that was all.

The energetic, good-looking young Vicar of St. Marks, the Reverend Andrew 'Andy' Evans, kept an eye on Kevin by visiting him in his home. This was the first Church that Andy had pastored following his ordination, so he valued the older man's wisdom and viewed him as a respected confidante. Privately, Kevin thought that Andy had a lot to learn, but acknowledged that he also was once a young, inexperienced theological graduate, and now quite liked being asked for advice.

Andy liked the relaxed atmosphere of Kevin's living area. It was filled with an assortment of old armchairs upholstered in anything from leather to English floral linen. They were warmed by the mahogany lustre of what he assumed was a piano.

Kevin always made a good pot of tea, and they both enjoyed using Margaret's teacups, as it seemed to taste better in those. On one such occasion, Andy confessed that his visit that morning was not entirely social.

'I wonder if you could help me with a big favour, Mr Lawrence. Please feel free to say no, though.'

He paused, as Kevin had gone into the kitchen briefly. The older man returned to the living room, the biscuit barrel in hand. Kevin stood there, where – as usual – he struggled to open the lid. Andy knew from past experience that an offer of help would be declined, but he sat forward on the edge of his chair, silently indicating for Kevin to hand over the offending container. His host just shook his head, gritted his teeth and, finally succeeding, sat down on his worn leather chair, handing his guest the barrel of biscuits.

With a word of thanks, Andy settled himself into a more comfortable position, munching on buttery shortbread while waiting for Kevin's go-ahead to continue.

'Fire away, young man. No harm in asking.'

Andy took a deep breath, being aware that he was expecting a lot from the fairly private elderly gentleman, but waded in regardless.

'Well, we've got a group of very challenging young boys here, who're really hard to get through to. Their ages are eleven to fourteen, so they shouldn't be hard to manage, but they are. We've tried doing some exciting things with them and for them, but I want them to start thinking of others too, as a means of looking beyond themselves and their own problems.'

'What kind of problems do they have?' asked Kevin, brushing crumbs from his thick pullover.

'Okay, nothing unusual for these days. The ones I'm aware of are shoplifting, being aggressive towards parents or a parent's new partner … Um …' Andy tried to read the old Vicar's face for any reaction, but Kevin simply kept stirring his tea. Andy cleared his throat and continued. 'Running away from home or school. Picking fights. Bullying – but that can be either dishing it out or receiving it. That sort of thing.'

'So, how do their group leaders feel about it all?' asked Kevin.

'They're determined to hang in there, even though the boys are making their lives a misery! The three of them are in their early twenties, and can get a bit discouraged at times. But the interesting thing is that the kids keep coming back each week, so they're doing a great job in the light of that alone.'

Kevin used a paper serviette to dab his thick moustache.

'Sounds like they need a bit of help, but where do I fit in with all this? Come on – out with it!'

'Well,' said the younger Vicar, 'you've probably seen a few of the kids about the place on a Sunday. They all seem to know who you are. You probably have no idea of what an identity you are at St. Marks. Anyway, because of that, I was wondering if we could set up some jobs for them to do around your garden or home. It would teach them a bit about service to others, and help them to feel good about themselves. As long as you don't expect perfection, I think it might achieve a really positive outcome. I'd arrange for the leaders to be here, too.'

Kevin closed his eyes and seemed deeply in thought, keeping his visitor waiting for a response. The wheels were turning, pros and cons. He'd become used to just quietly attending Sunday services, then going home. This would mean opening his home up again on a regular basis.

Andy was wriggling in his chair, biting his lip, drumming on the armrest, and looking at the ceiling like a restless schoolboy in trouble.

Kevin looked seriously toward the fidgety man seated opposite. Then mischievously, with a twinkle in his eye, he smiled.

'Yes, I'll be in it. Margaret and I had four children and ran youth groups, so I've got experience to draw upon. You'll have to let me be pretty firm with them, though. I'll give them a bit of a lecture before they start. No use beating about the bush with stuff like this!'

Andy sighed with relief, reached across the coffee table and shook his friend's hand with sincere thanks.

***

By the following Saturday, group leaders Josh, Jenna and Jack, along with their young charges, gathered in Kevin's front room. Quite a few boys were crossing their arms defensively, seeming uncomfortable, reluctant or sullen. In contrast, the old Vicar's confident posture, no-nonsense air and almost military demeanour gave an impression of authority.

'Right-oh, lads!' Kevin began. He used this call when wanting to gain a group's attention, when instructing them, praising them, taking them to task, or giving them a break. *They'll learn it soon enough,* he thought.

Before he could continue, one young fellow separated from the group and headed straight for the pianola. He lifted the lid and started to bang away on the keys discordantly, at an ear-piercing volume.

Despite Kevin's bothersome knees, he was at the boy's side in two seconds, with a steely glare. The ill-mannered boy, returned the glare, and slammed down the lid in a fit of rage. Sensing he wouldn't win this battle, the boy clomped back to his mates with a curse word directed at Kevin. Unfazed, the cleric ploughed on.

'Right-oh, lads! This is how it's going to be at my place,' he said firmly.

He didn't give anyone the chance to act up further, laying down the law to the group right from the start, including respecting his property, and no swearing.

'Right-oh, lads,' he said once more after he'd finished the brief introduction. 'Come with me. I've got quite a few things to show you now.'

His tone of voice suggested that the idea of disobedience had never crossed his mind!

Mumbling, the straggly team nevertheless followed him outside as Josh, Jenna and Jack accompanied them to inspect the front and back garden. Moving quickly from place to place, Kevin demonstrated weeding, trimming, fertilizing, repotting, edging and watering, but then stood back so they could try doing it for themselves.

The boys were allowed to choose their own tasks. One older boy, named Ben, wanted to mow the front and back lawns, but the leaders were worried about safety.

'That's not fair! At home I do it all the time,' he complained, wanting to impress the others with his ability.

Kevin whispered to Jenna, 'Are you insured?' to which she nodded in reply.

He was certain that nobody could start his pesky mower anyway, so made a suggestion.

'Perhaps you'd like to demonstrate its parts, Ben, and then describe how you operate it, since the old girl's on her last legs, I'm afraid. But if you can get it going, the job's yours. Stand back, everyone.'

It started for Ben the first time. He was the hero of the hour and Kevin finished up with a nice neat lawn.

Kevin moved around the group for all of the allocated time. He had a way of teaching new skills one-to-one, in a way that kept the lads interested and engaged. Even the boy he'd had the run-in with earlier asked him a question without attitude and took note of the answer.

Andy dropped by later that day, after officiating at a wedding. The boys proudly walked him around the garden, showing him what they'd achieved. As thanks for work surprisingly well done, Kevin handed out some icy-poles.

'Thanks, Mr Lawrence,' said a few of the boys.

Kevin cupped his ear, feigning deafness.

'What did you say?'

'Thanks, Mr Lawrence!' most of them shouted back.

After slurping and dripping melting icy-poles onto the newly-mown lawn, they were soon sprawling all over it or chasing Josh, Jenna and Jack, to let off some steam.

After the boys had gone home Andy quizzed Kevin, as they were still in shock that every hard-to-handle boy had stayed on the job until home time.

'It's no great secret,' the old man explained. 'I just made sure that I moved around to each boy, working alongside them. It's well documented that males communicate or confide best when they're working with their hands, side by side. So even in that short time, some of them dropped their guard. Three of them told me about significant problems at home or school. They're good lads.'

***

Before too long, the boys were knocking on Kevin's door once a fortnight, choosing jobs from his list and then, when completed, enthusiastically fronting up for more. Kevin,

Josh, Jenna and Jack chatted alongside them as they worked, praised the boys' efforts, and offered help if they wanted it. The adults knew how to show an interest in their personal problems without prying, but the boys determined if and when they were ready to open up.

One day, a hardworking little chap called Timothy stopped Kevin as they passed the pianola. He looked up appealingly and asked, 'Could you teach me to play your piano please, Mr Lawrence?'

'No, I'm sorry, Timothy. I've never learnt to play. But, I can teach you a great trick! Just hold on a moment.' Kevin put a finger to his lips with a 'Shh' as he chose one of the rolls from a cabinet. He quickly set it up in its cavity, ready to be played.

Timothy, with eyes gleaming, enjoyed being part of some kind of secret, noting with fascination every move Kevin made.

The old trickster closed the little wooden doors that covered the roll then walked to the back door of the house.

'Right-oh, lads!' he called out to the young workers. 'Time for a break. I need you back here.'

Boots and shoes were thrown into a pile at the back door as the boys gathered around the pianola in the lounge room.

'Now,' Kevin began, 'young Timothy was asking about learning to play this beautiful instrument. He's never had a lesson, but I'll bet he can play it in just a few minutes!' he teased.

The group's curiosity aroused, Kevin quietly instructed the boy to perch on the slanted wooden stool, grip the underside of the keyboard, pedal hard and evenly, but not too fast. After a shaky start, he soon got the idea, and everyone, especially Timothy, was fascinated as the keys moved up and down, and the sounds of upbeat music poured out as though it were a normal piano. No one seemed to mind that it was a slightly out of tune!

The small boy's glowing, smiley face was a sight to behold, as he moved his fingers up and down the keyboard, pretending to play.

The others leaned in, trying to fathom how it was all happening. When the last verse was about to start, Kevin opened the little doors to reveal how the paper roll moved, so they could all see the words of the verse printed down the side of the paper. He started to sing, then, turning around with a smile, encouraging the group to sing along with him.

Soon, these supposedly troublesome boys were joining in, right up to the big ending! Once the song was over, they all clamoured around, wanting their turn to play next. The songs were changed over to different ones. Not all of them were familiar to the boys, but they learned fast.

Kevin absorbed what was happening. Not all of the boys could sing in tune, but that didn't matter. They made up for it in enthusiasm! These were lads who may not have known this kind of fun with music before. No embarrassment, no competition, no microphones, no teachers or judges critiquing their performance, no marks out of ten. No lewd lyrics either! Surprisingly, he could sense no embarrassment from the boys about doing something uncool in front of their mates.

Before anyone knew, it was nearly time for them to be collected to go home. Kevin asked everyone to join together in singing the Lord's Prayer, with the eldest boy playing it on the pianola.

The jovial mood of the previous hour calmed, as the boys concentrated on tackling the unfamiliar classical tune, guessing correctly that a degree of reverence was expected.

'I know that one,' Timothy called out. 'My Grandma from Scotland used to sing it.'

Timothy's young voice ascended above all the others, and they soon fell away, listening to him carrying on his grandmother's tradition of singing that beautiful song (with just a hint of Scottish accent!). Timothy wasn't aware of how thoughtfully he sang. He just remembered how his Grandma had sung it.

There was no applause for him, just an awed, appreciative hush. This was followed by some words of encouragement, thanks, and a little blessing for each boy from the old Vicar before they went home.

Not much work was completed that day, but the group had bonded wonderfully. In the previous weeks, they'd learnt about respect for the elderly, for their youth leaders, for each other, and even for themselves.

***

The two clerics were soon chatting once again over a cuppa in Kevin's home. This time, the Monte Carlo biscuits skated across the bench when the biscuit barrel's stubborn owner suddenly released its contents. Andy pretended not to notice and looked elsewhere, studying a fine watercolour hanging on the opposite wall.

The usual niceties always included a report on Kevin's robust state of health. He preferred to ignore the problem with his knees, so it was never mentioned.

Today, Kevin had a new subject to discuss. It was his turn to feel unsure about how his news would be received. Procrastination seemed to be the best way to start.

'How's your tea, Andy?' he asked. 'Can I pour you another one? Help yourself to more biscuits. I can get you some cheese ones if you'd like something more savoury.'

Andy politely declined. 'You seem to have something on your mind, Mr Lawrence,' he said, intrigued. 'I can keep a confidence too, you know.'

'No, sorry,' Kevin smiled in response. 'I've got no shameful transgressions to divulge. It's just that I've been thinking about the pianola. Seeing what a hit it was with the lads, I've decided that I'd like to donate it to the groups who use the Church hall, but they'd need to raise money for the proper repairs needed. I could put something towards that, but not much, I'm afraid. I wondered if the other youth groups might have fun trundling it across the road, to save on moving costs or perhaps …'

Kevin stopped speaking as he watched Andy's head slowly move from side to side. The old Vicar's offer was being rejected. Again. He thought that the young Vicar would have known that the instrument held precious memories for him, and would have let him down more sensitively. Deflated, Kevin's bushy eyebrows converged into a frown.

'No,' Andy said forcefully, jumping up, stepping around to the back of his chair, and leaning his arms on it as though it were a pulpit. 'That's a very touching and generous offer, Mr Lawrence. Honestly, I'm very grateful, but I'm telling you now, it's not moving from your place here. You can put it in your will that it should go to our Church if you like, but while you're on this earth, the pianola stays right here. And we'll have it fixed, because the boys, and hopefully a few more visitors, are going to want to keep on enjoying it, with your permission.'

Kevin looked puzzled but relieved, and asked why the cleric was so vehement.

Returning to his chair, Andy smiled, wondering whether to open up or not. He was surprised that Kevin hadn't seen through his plan.

'Mr Lawrence,' he explained gently, 'you're a Vicar with a pastor's heart. You really do care about everyone. I've been told that you and Margaret made a wonderful team, with your obvious love for each other and warm hospitality, but you fell in a heap after she passed away.'

Andy paused as Kevin drew out his handkerchief and began polishing his glasses.

'I'm not saying that you haven't made a contribution,' Andy continued. 'I've really appreciated your input since I arrived, personally speaking. You've been pretty courageous, really, but until the kids invaded your space, you'd been going to Church, but avoiding spending any more time with people than you absolutely had to, when it's obvious that people are your speciality.'

The older man couldn't believe the younger one's perception and insight. Andy really summed up how it had been over the past three years. Kevin let Andy continue.

'Mr Lawrence, the friends that you and Margaret made here are missing you and have been concerned about you, so I hatched a plan to open up your big heart again and get those kids involved in your life. It was meant to benefit them, but you as well. And it's worked, hasn't it? You've had a great time with those kids, especially when you introduced them to the pianola. They've changed for the better, but so have you. There's a bit of a spring in your step now, which is great to see.'

Kevin shook his head at Andy's big reveal, and smiled.

'You put one over me, you young whipper-snapper!' he declared. 'Maybe you boys and girls just out of college aren't as green as I thought. Salutations to you, Reverend Evans! You've got bucketsful of what it takes. You're a fine pastor. Oh! And please call me Kevin. But not Kev and not Rev, and certainly not Rev Kev! At least not when I'm within earshot!'

Andy laughed and Kevin continued enthusiastically.

'Andy, while I've got your ear, I think your little experiment could be repeated with other people, too. And not only with oldies like me, but perhaps single parents, or parents looking after children with special needs, or anyone living with a disability. In fact, anyone who could use a hand. If the older teens and young adults came on board, we could help quite a lot. I'd be willing to get it off the ground. And then there's this business of what's been happening at the shopping centre ...'

'Whoa! Steady on, old man. We only have twenty-four hours in each day, you know!'

Kevin grinned. 'And I'm not going to waste however many I have left!'

***

A few days later, a parcel was delivered to the Reverend Lawrence's door. He opened it to find an attractive pottery biscuit barrel with a wide, loose lid that easily lifted from a groove at the top. The card with familiar bold handwriting read:

> *Huge thanks for all your hospitality, Kevin. Please boil the kettle on Thursday at 10:30, as usual. There's work to be done!*

Service with a Smile

'We're getting close to Mr Bell's place now, Jan.' Polly leaned forward in the front passenger seat of the little blue car, peering through her stylish glasses at the houses on her left. 'It's number fifteen. I'm glad you're behind the wheel, Jan – some of these houses look all the same. Whoops! We've gone past it. You'll need to do a U-ie.'

The car slowed to a stop at the side of the street. Even though she had first-day jitters, Jan, the driver, had shown that she had the presence of mind to brake carefully. There were many containers of hot food in the back, and she didn't want stalactites of meat sauce dripping from the underside of her car's roof!

'I'll just need a moment,' Jan said, pausing to regain her composure. Looking back toward the houses they'd passed, she asked, 'Is it the cream weatherboard one, or the red brick, Polly?'

'The red brick one, darl. The one with pots of geraniums lined up along the verandah. I'm glad that the flowers are there, or I'd never find it.'

As the road along the nature strip was free of parked cars, Jan simply reversed until they stopped outside Mr Bell's house.

Jan's passenger, Polly, was well into her senior years. She had been delivering meals to the elderly for almost four decades. The meals program was run by the Municipal Council, as a means of looking after their aged ratepayers. The Council provided the premises, where insulated containers of freshly cooked, nutritious three-course meals were prepared by volunteers. They were then delivered to each home by other kind-hearted volunteers like Polly and Jan.

Jan opened up the hatchback. She carried the heavier container of food, while Polly took the lighter one. It was then that Jan noticed Polly's knobbly arthritic fingers.

'Can you manage that, Polly?' she asked.

'Sure!' the older woman replied. 'I'm not going to let a bit of osteo slow me down! I'm just glad my legs are no trouble.'

Jan loved Polly's positive attitude.

They walked toward the front door.

'Just put down the esky and knock on the door for me, will you, darl?' she said, which Jan proceeded to do. 'Oh! And we've got to hand over one of these envelopes from the Council today, along with the food. My guess is that it'll be about a price rise. Probably just a small one, but to pensioners especially, it'll be an added expense that they just don't need.'

Jan's private thought was that there had to be a better way, but she just kept her opinion to herself. Until that moment, she'd thought that the recipients didn't have to pay anything.

After a minute or two, the door was opened by a cheerful Mr Bell. He ushered them down a hallway, stopping at his kitchen table. Jan was introduced and the envelope handed over, while all three unpacked his meal. He sniffed the air with exaggerated appreciation, and thanked them both.

With a twinkle in his eye, he said, 'Have you heard the one about the frog, the Priest, the Rabbi and the Lawyer? They played golf every–'

'–Sorry, Mr Bell,' Polly interrupted. 'You'll have to save our joke 'til next week! We're behind time today. I'm breaking in a new driver!' Polly nodded towards Jan.

'I'll have to get two yarns ready for next time then,' he threatened impishly, pointing a finger at Polly. 'That'll serve you right!'

'Oh, no! What've we done to deserve that?' Polly called out, as the laughing women left.

'You'd never know he was ninety-four, would you?' said Polly, as they loaded up the car.

Jan was amazed, mainly because of his happy, youthful outlook. As they drove to the next house, Polly quizzed her new partner.

'So, why is a young girl like you delivering meals for the oldies? We don't get many volunteers at your age, but I'm glad that you're here, just the same.'

'Well, I'm married with three boys, and the youngest one has just started school,' Jan replied. 'We can manage on one income, so I'm free to do something else during school hours.'

'Goodness me! You could be doing aerobics or meeting girlfriends for coffee.'

'Well, I do like a catch-up for coffee now and then, but you'd be surprised, Polly. A few of my friends volunteer their time here and there and not only at their children's school either.'

'Well, I'm glad you told me that. I suppose I was your age when I started doing this, too. I love the people I see and I promise you will too.'

At the next stop, Jan met a tall, thin lady who took ages to come to the door. When she appeared, she was wearing the tell-tale headscarf of a cancer patient who'd been receiving chemotherapy.

'Look, Polly! I've got hair again!' she said excitedly, pulling back the colourful scarf to show a hint of pearly-white growth.

'I bet you it'll come back curly as it grows longer,' Polly said. 'Mine did, both times!'

Jan swallowed, and tried not to look too shocked at learning this bit of news about Polly.

When they returned to the car, Jan couldn't keep quiet any longer. 'Polly,' she began to ask, 'how many times have you had a course of chemo? That is, if you don't mind me asking,' Jan quickly added, keeping her eyes firmly on the road ahead.

'That's fine to ask,' Polly replied. 'Well, it's been three times at last count, but my hair just thinned first time around. I was totally bald after the other two bouts, though. It's cancer, of course, but I keep bouncing back. I won't go into detail, but I'm in remission once again, so I'm very glad about that.'

'You're amazing! You must get tired, though. Have you ever wondered if you should give away the food deliveries for good?'

'No, never,' Polly replied. 'I've got every reason to keep going! Why do you think I'm still in this world? I see all these people who're mostly housebound, a lot living on their own. I've still got my husband, my family and friends, and I can get out and about. I count my blessings every day. I would never give it away willingly. I love this little job.'

Jan nodded, knowing she meant every word.

The long delivery round with its lovely people continued, with Polly's cheeriness making it a real pleasure, but there were heart-wrenching moments, too. Such as when they spoke to a man who was usually accompanied by his wife. He said he'd only need one meal in future, not two. At another house, a district nurse who answered the door for a very ill gentleman said he was going to a hospice and didn't expect to return home. Polly would be reporting those sad occurrences to the manager, so that professional care and support could be offered.

For a moment, the women sat quietly in the car, processing what they'd been told at the last two houses.

'I'm sorry I couldn't meet the man who was going to the hospice,' said Jan. 'And I just wanted to stay and talk to that beautiful man whose wife had died, so I could give him a big hug.'

'I know how you feel, Jan,' Polly agreed. 'But our job is to get a good hot meal to a whole lot of people – we can't let our feelings slow us down and we can't forget how important these meals are. Without them, many people would go into care when they often want to stay in their own homes for as long as possible. We've got to keep on the move.'

The deliveries continued, until they arrived at the last house on their list. Polly told Jan about the sweet lady she'd meet there, as they walked down a long path, carrying the food toward the front door of her clinker brick house.

'The woman's name is Mrs Rowland. She lives alone and is quite fragile.'

Before they could ring the bell, the small woman opened the door to welcome her visitors. She thanked them profusely for coming, as was always her custom. After unpacking the three courses and briefly checking on how she was health-wise, the two volunteers left, and started their return drive back to the depot.

'Oh, no!' said Jan, suddenly. 'We didn't give her one of those letters from the Council!'

'We'd better go back,' said Polly. 'It's only a couple of kilometres. I'm glad you remembered.'

'Polly, is that your real name, or is it a nickname?' Jan asked as they cruised along. 'It's not short for Pollyanna, is it?'

'It is and it isn't!' replied Polly, chuckling. 'You've guessed quicker than anyone else ever has. Yes, it's a nickname that they gave me at the meals kitchen. Apparently, I say "glad" a lot, just like Pollyanna from the children's book. She would always play "the glad game". So the name stuck. I'm glad that it's from Pollyanna, though. I used to love that book.'

'I think it suits you,' Jan commented with a smile.

'I don't mind it myself. I'm glad it's Polly, and not Brunhilda, or Medea, or worse still, my real name!' Taking turns to think of unattractive names, they were still laughing as the little car pulled up at Mrs Rowland's house for the second time that afternoon.

Grabbing the forgotten envelope, Polly said, 'I'll quickly take it in. You just keep the engine running, darl. I won't take long.'

She ran with surprising agility and prepared to call out at the front door. It was a beautifully warm day, so the door was wide open and Polly could easily see through it to the dining table.

'It's Polly again, Mrs Rowland. Don't get up. I'll just let myself in,' she announced, stepping just inside the doorway.

There to her right, sitting at a table complete with a pretty cloth, sat a slight elderly male, his back facing Polly. He was ploughing into the delivered dinner, with gusto! The empty fine china bowl was evidence the soup was finished. The enticing dessert sat close at hand.

Mrs Rowland sat at the other end of the table, with a cup of tea and a piece of toast. As soon as she saw Polly, she came to the door, a finger to her lips. She beckoned Polly outside.

'Mrs Rowland,' Polly spoke first, 'why is that man eating your lunch? It's meant to be for you. Does this happen all the time?'

'Don't be cross with me, Polly,' the dear lady appealed, shamefaced. 'It's the man next door. His wife was my best friend. Before she died, I promised her that I'd make sure he ate properly after she was gone. I used to cook him a good

'Don't be cross with me, Polly.'

lunch, but I can't do that anymore. I know for sure that he can't afford the delivered meals, and I can't afford to put in a second order, so I always put the meal you bring onto my own china, and he's none the wiser. He thinks I cooked it all myself.'

'But what about you, Mrs Rowland?'

'I'm happy with some toast for lunch. I just tell him I'm saving my main meal for teatime.'

'Well, you seem to have thought of everything, haven't you? Don't worry, you won't be in trouble. I must go. I've got a notice for you here, but that can wait until next week. Bye!'

Polly quickly tucked the Council envelope in her handbag and walked back to the car. Mrs Rowland's secret wasn't mentioned on the drive back to the depot.

The following week, Jan and Polly were told that two meals were to be delivered to Mrs Rowland's address in future, and to simply tell her that she now qualified for two meals, free of charge.

'I wonder why?' Jan said. Polly feigned ignorance. Sensing that Polly knew much more than she was revealing, Jan gave a wry smile. 'That's very generous of the management, isn't it? I'm glad, so very, very glad that they've got a heart after all.'

Too Good to be True?

Carolyn Webb had a secret. Although it was nothing shameful, the sadness it brought had hung over her life like a grey veil.

In all of her sixty-two years she had never been asked out on a date.

As a young adult, she had despaired about her lack of a boyfriend as, one by one, her closest friends married and had children. In private, she'd often wondered if there was something wrong with her personality, but felt that her interactions with others would be considered normal. Regarding her appearance, she had been quietly confident that her slender figure and ash-blonde hair would be seen as assets. Finding no apparent reason for still being single, reluctant acceptance of her fate came gradually.

In conversation, she had never raised the subject, not even with her best friend, Wendy.

To Carolyn, it was too personal, too painful. It seemed that something she had dreamed about as a child was never to be.

Wendy understood that her friend was a very private person, so she didn't pry. However, that didn't stop her from expressing concern with a couple of mutual friends. In Carolyn's absence, they had occasionally tried to set her up with men they knew, but there were no takers, and therefore, no dates.

'I don't understand it,' said Wendy, who could see nothing but good in her friend. 'Carrie's a lovely person, and still very attractive. She can hold an interesting conversation, and always considers the other person's point of view. Men don't know what they're missing.'

Their friends, Bev and Jill, could only agree as they pooled their ideas.

'Do you think she might seem almost too good to be true?' asked Bev.

'You could be right,' agreed Jill. 'Maybe men feel they could never live up to her high standards of behaviour.'

'I think it's because she doesn't want to seem flirty,' added Wendy. 'I've never seen her liven up when she's talking to anyone eligible, so men don't get the usual feedback. I suppose we should just accept that Carrie's Mr Right may never appear.'

***

Throughout a friendship spanning over four decades, the three friends and their husbands had made sure that Carolyn was an important part of their families' social lives. They had never made any distinction simply because she was single. She was affectionately known to their children as 'Auntie Carrie'. They played games with her and confided in her as they navigated adolescence. After the children grew up and left home, the parents had more time to themselves. One Saturday every month the group of seven would arrange to go out together. Carolyn was, of course, one of the seven.

She was happy to attend these events solo or, now and then, with a friend of either gender. She varied those she invited along, as her old friends enjoyed meeting some new and different people.

On one of these monthly occasions, Carolyn brought along her neighbour, Don Lloyd. They'd been on good terms for years, but the friendship had never gone beyond collecting the mail if one was on holiday, or a few minutes of conversation at a front fence. He'd been a particularly quiet man until more recently, when he'd grown in confidence and had become much more outgoing. Carolyn put that down to changing his IT job to a new one – also in IT – at

National Football Headquarters. Carolyn knew that asking him to accompany her was a bold step, but he agreed to come along.

As the group outing was at the movies, no one had much of a chance to talk to Don. Standing in the foyer afterwards, they all chatted for a short time. When the time came for some much-needed coffee, Carolyn and Don declined, leaving earlier than the others.

In the coffee lounge, Wendy asked, 'So, what did you think of Don?'

'We really didn't have a chance to get to know him, did we?' said Bev.

'Not really,' agreed Jill. 'But there was something about him that I like, and it's not just those dark brown eyes and silvery hair. No, to me he just seemed like a really decent chap.'

The others could only agree, but didn't expect to see him again, as that was Carolyn's usual pattern with the platonic friends who accompanied her.

The following month's get-together was at a pancake restaurant. The girls' eyes lit up as Carolyn was, again, escorted by Don. After all eight were seated, and orders placed for a scrumptious range of pancakes, the conversation flowed.

Don mixed comfortably within the group without drawing attention to himself. The girls' husbands enjoyed talking footy with him, because he'd met quite a few players in his workplace. The wives liked his pleasant manner, noting the positive effect it had on Carolyn. When in his company, she seemed more relaxed, smiling and laughing. The three girlfriends could hardly contain their excitement when the couple left, hand in hand, at the end of the evening.

'I think Don could be *the one*,' said an elated Wendy, as they shared their observations over cappuccinos. 'Did you notice how animated Carrie seemed when they were talking together?'

'I certainly did!' replied Jill. 'She was almost flirting! I've never seen her behave like that in her whole life. I hear wedding bells!'

Jill's husband reprimanded the women for predicting Carolyn's future so soon, and on the basis of such thin evidence.

Wendy made a forecast. 'It wouldn't surprise me if they were married within twelve months. They'd want to make the most of their remaining years together.'

'Yes, none of us are spring chickens anymore,' said Bev. 'But I'm going to reserve judgement. Anyone who's so presentable, and still unattached at his age, must have some sort of baggage from the past. He seems too good to be true.'

***

The four girlfriends had first met in their late teens, while working at Nightingales, a busy city bridal store. Around forty years had passed. Carolyn continued to work there, making her way up to the position of Manager of the ground floor showroom, while her friends interrupted their careers to raise their families. As their children grew, each woman had returned to work in the business they loved.

It was not surprising when Carolyn asked her three friends to start work an hour earlier on the Monday following their visit to the pancake restaurant. She greeted them at the door, as they ambled through to the front showroom, carrying their usual take-away lattes. Carolyn locked the doors behind them. Walking to the centre of the parquetry floor, she extended her arm in an arc, pointing toward the bride's and bridesmaids' gowns on display.

'I need you to help me pick out a range of possibilities, girls. There's a quickie morning wedding coming up in less than a month, so we need to allow time for alterations after the dresses are tried on. We need one bride's outfit and three attendants. They're all mature women, so they'll need something that—'

A loud squeal came from Jill. Her eyes had caught the flash of a diamond ring on Carolyn's left hand.

Excitedly, Carolyn announced, 'Yes, we're engaged! I'm in love! Don's swept me off my feet!'

The lattes were speedily put aside as laughter, hugs and admiration of the lovely ring followed. Finally, the pandemonium settled. Carolyn first ascertained if her girlfriends could be her attendants in only three weeks' time. Of course, they happily agreed.

'So that's why we're here!' exclaimed Wendy.

'Yes, and I'm hoping you'll help me to find the right outfit, too. We're planning a church wedding at eleven, so I don't want anything too glittery. We're hoping that the reception will be a sit-down luncheon in a marquee at my place. There's not enough time to book anywhere else.'

'That sounds perfect, Carrie,' said Bev, 'but why the big rush? You must be pregnant! Sounds like a shotgun wedding to me!'

The three women laughed again, but stopped when they noticed that Carolyn wasn't laughing.

'Why should they wait, Bev?' Wendy quickly changed the subject, realising such a flippant remark could still be hurtful for someone whose child-bearing years were over. 'They're in love! I think it's just wonderful.' She wandered around the huge room, trying to remember where some of her favourite bridesmaids' dresses were hanging.

'So romantic,' added Jill, as she carried the lattes into a side room, to avoid spills on the beautiful fabrics.

'Yes, it really is,' agreed Carolyn. 'After all these years, the love of my life was the nice man living two doors away! But there's a practical reason for our haste, too. Don had already arranged to take a bit of leave before I came on the scene,' she explained. 'He'd paid an airfare for a New Zealand holiday, so that's why we're rushing things a bit. He's paid for two tickets now – oops!' she grinned cheekily. 'We're supposed to keep the honeymoon destination a secret, aren't we?' she asked, pressing a finger to her lips.

'We won't tell,' Wendy promised. 'Now, let's get down to choosing your outfit, Carrie. What do you have in mind? After that, you can help us choose ours.'

The four fashion advisors soon reached agreement on calf-length gowns that they all loved. The bride-to-be chose a stunning garment of soft lilac with a beaded lace overlay. Her friends selected three different styles, but each in the same silvery-grey crepe. All four women chose elegant little hats as finishing touches, leaving them delighted with the resulting effect. All of this was achieved in the allocated hour before the shop opened for business.

***

After working hours, Carolyn's leisure time was filled with the rest of the wedding planning. She was a habitual writer of 'To Do' lists, and enjoyed the feeling of achievement each time she ticked a completed task.

The most urgent item on her list was invitations. Because there were only three weeks from engagement to marriage, there could be no formal cards sent in the mail six weeks beforehand, as was the tradition. Although it irked her to resort to phone calls, it certainly saved time. Everyone was delighted by the engagement news, and even more so by the verbal wedding invitation. Almost all replied with a 'yes' before the phone calls ended.

Gradually, neat ticks appeared next to the many other items on her list. Don was an obliging fiancé. Every time that Carolyn needed to discuss plans, he made himself available. He soon learned that agreeing to almost everything made the whole process easier!

***

It was a Friday evening, eight days before the wedding. Don was in Carolyn's kitchen, pouring cups of tea after enjoying a delicious home-cooked meal. His other contribution had been to mash the potatoes – a new experience for him! He placed the cups and saucers on a tray, and carried it to the living room coffee table, next to where Carolyn was relaxing on the couch.

'Weak tea, no milk, half a teaspoon of sugar. Right?' Don asked. She nodded and thanked him as he passed it to her. 'Carolyn,' he started, as he settled himself next to her. 'I've been wondering if we might be rushing all this a bit too much. You're doing a great job with planning the wedding, but we haven't discussed very much about our life after the honeymoon yet.'

Carolyn was taken aback. Her trembling hands couldn't stop the teacup rattling in its saucer. 'What are you trying to tell me, Don? Do you want to break off the engagement?' she asked, despite being afraid of what his answer could be.

'No, darling girl,' he replied with a reassuring smile. 'I'd never do that. Can't wait til I see you walking down the aisle.'

Carolyn gave a sigh of relief. Don drew her closer on the couch, placing his arm around her shoulder. 'It's just that I'd like to know your thoughts about all kinds of things. We're both working now, but it'd be nice to talk about what we'd like to do in retirement, for instance. I'd like to buy a small boat, so we could go fishing along the east coast. Maybe we could join the grey nomads and caravan around Australia. I like the outdoors. I believe it's a mistake to stop work without some kind of plan.'

Carolyn thought it best not to mention how she suffered from seasickness.

'At one stage, I'd wondered about running a B&B, but I don't think I've got the stamina for it now,' she confided. 'Apart from that, I haven't put much thought into retirement at all. Since your proposal, I've only wondered about what side of the bed you'd like, and how we're going to share the housework.'

'Oh, don't worry about that,' Don said. 'We'll work it out. I can't cook, but I'll stack the dishwasher. Is that the sort of thing you mean?'

Having visited his unit, Carolyn guessed that stacking the dishwasher might be his only domestic skill! Perhaps he needed to be taught a little more than how to mash potatoes! She looked at the clock, surprised that it showed a quarter to eleven.

'Goodness! Look at the time! I'm going to have to send you home, Don. Sorry, dear, but you won't be doing this for much longer. After we marry, this will be your home, too.'

'And then we can both tumble into bed any time we like!' Don whispered. Carolyn smiled shyly.

He respected Carolyn's wish to save further intimacy until the honeymoon, so, hand in hand, they arose from the couch and slowly walked to the front door. With fond farewell kisses on the doorstep, their relaxing Friday night together ended.

***

Carolyn awoke the following morning with the sudden realisation that there was now only one week to go until the big day!

'There's no need for panic,' she told herself. The couple had arranged everything they could thus far, including the outfits for Don and his groomsmen. Professionals would take care of the remaining details on the Friday and early Saturday morning.

Carolyn pulled on a pair of jeans, loose top and sandals. As she did, she couldn't help running through her mental checklist: *Hairdressing. Orders of service and flowers for the church. Four bouquets and four buttonholes for the wedding party. Two more for the ushers. Photography. Chauffeured cars. House cleaning. Setting up the marquee for the caterers and musicians. Packing up and more cleaning afterwards.*

Don had insisted on paying others for the cleaning services, so that they could really enjoy their once-in-a-lifetime day. Carolyn was grateful. Her head was spinning just thinking of it all! Wanting to clear her mind, she grabbed the car keys and left the house.

As she drove away, the preparations were still uppermost in her mind. She recalled that the kindly church minister had already chatted with Don and herself about the meaning of the marriage service, and their commitment to each other. It was a significant conversation, but she'd hardly given it a second thought since then.

Don was right, I really have let wedding plans crowd out other important matters.

Carolyn drove up to her favourite place for breakfast: a small out-of-the-way seaside café at the end of a short row of shops. The girl at the register recognised her as an occasional Saturday morning customer.

'Now, let me see,' she said. 'A ham, cheese and spinach omelette, cappuccino, and a newspaper. Am I close?'

'You're exactly right! I'm impressed,' said Carolyn. Solving crosswords in the newspaper was part of every morning's quiet routine, whether at home or elsewhere. She started the cryptic one while waiting for the food to arrive.

A thought struck her from out of the blue. *What if Don likes noise at brekky time?* Carolyn could think of nothing worse. She knew that a lot of people had the radio or television blaring first thing in the morning. Her own calm start to the day was important to her. Would she have to give it up? Was she too set in her ways to do so?

Somewhat rattled, the bride-to-be allowed her thoughts to wander along those lines as she ate her breakfast and left the café. She walked back to her car, sat in the front passenger seat and foraged in the glove box for her notebook and pen. Sitting in the warmth of the morning sun, she started to write.

Carolyn rapidly journaled her concerns and doubts that seemed to come from nowhere. She wrote that when she was younger, her future dreams had always centred on marriage and family. She'd seen her single state as second best, almost as a fall-back position, but now that she was getting married, she knew she was going to miss her independence. For the first time, Carolyn realised how much she loved her single life.

She wrote about the pressure and exhaustion she felt in arranging a marriage so quickly. Working in the bridal shop had certainly helped her to know the procedure but, as Don said, those plans left little time to talk about their future. How could she know if they had much in common, if they hardly knew each other? And so it continued. She filled seven large pages without having to try very hard at all.

On the drive home, some well-known words echoed in her head.

Marry in haste, repent at leisure.

***

The moment Carolyn returned home from the beach, her telephone rang. Slinging her laden bag onto the kitchen bench, she answered it.

'How's my sweetheart today?' came Don's cheerful voice at the end of the line.

'Oh, not bad, I guess,' Carolyn faltered. 'Perhaps a bit nervous about next Saturday.'

Don could hear the anxiety in her voice. 'Do you think we could go for a drive somewhere this afternoon, dear? It would give us a chance to talk some more.'

'Yes, why not?' she replied agreeably, while trying to hide a sense of foreboding.

'Great,' he said, sounding relieved. 'It might cure your collywobbles. Perhaps we could make it a mystery destination. Don't dress up. Let's just make it a nice, relaxing afternoon. What time would you like me to pick you up?'

'If we make it half past two, it would give me a chance for a little nap after lunch. Do you ever do that?' Carolyn asked, stifling a yawn.

'Yes, I never miss a snooze on the weekends. Can't wait 'til I can have them during the week, too. See you at two-thirty. Bye for now. Love you.'

'Love you, too,' Carolyn replied, somewhat less confidently, as the many concerns written in her notebook were uppermost in her mind.

After the phone call, she thought, *at least liking a nap after lunch is one thing we have in common!*

***

The drive around nearby hills with their lovely vistas was refreshing. Don had just replaced his broken car radio with a nice new one. It was tuned to a classic FM station. That was a surprise to Carolyn.

'Do you play this music at home, or is it just to impress me?' she asked.

'You're funny, Carolyn. No, what you see is what you get. I hate jarring music. What kind do you like?'

'I love the classics as well, but there's a station that plays smooth ballads and some quieter popular songs that I like. It's just nice to have it on in the background sometimes. I think you'd like it, too.'

'Well, be my guest! Can you find it with the search button? If I'm ever going to be open to new experiences, it's now.'

Carolyn's worry about Don's musical tastes dissipated in an instant. Before she'd left home, she'd ripped out the seven pages of journaling from her notebook. They were safely folded in the pocket of the summery floral dress she was wearing. Throughout the relaxed drive, she casually wove into the conversation some of the concerns and questions she'd written down. She was pleased with many of his responses, a little disappointed by others, but this led to talking about a variety of subjects, and opening up to each other in a way that they never had before.

'I'm really enjoying this drive, sweetheart,' Don commented. 'I feel as though I'm really getting to know my bride at last. I like what I'm hearing. I can't believe that I've found you, when I've been so unlucky with women in the past.'

'Why do you think you haven't had much success?' Carolyn asked. 'To me, you're the best.'

Don paused, looking at the road intently. 'Darling, I told you I'd been a bachelor all my life, but I should've explained why,' he said with a husky voice. 'The fact is, that until fairly recently, I suffered from the effects of an abusive childhood. My bullying father left me with zero self-confidence, and women were turned off by that. But there was another thing that they didn't like. I swore I'd never be a father. I had no experience of a healthy father-child relationship, so I wasn't going to inflict poor modelling on a child of my own.'

Carolyn paled. She asked Don to park the car. He slowed to a stop inside the entrance to a park. They undid their seatbelts and snuggled together, watching a flock of screeching green parrots swooping above the trees.

'Oh Don, I'm so sorry. I had no idea,' Carolyn said, gently. 'Would you mind telling me more, or is it too painful?'

'It *was* painful when I was just a little bloke,' Don recalled. 'Dad beat me with the buckle end of his thick belt, or anything else within reach. I wasn't athletic like my brothers and sisters, so he tried to toughen me up, I suppose. He kept doing it until he died when I was fourteen.'

'Don, you're amazing. I can't imagine how you survived all that cruelty! Thank you for telling me, darling. But to me, you seem so comfortable in your own skin. How did you recover from all that?'

'About three years ago, I finally saw a very good psychologist who helped me turn my life around. Dad used to say hideous things about me, yelling his lies right into my face, and I believed him, because I was just a kid. The psychologist helped me to see how he messed with my head, so after a lifetime of self-loathing, I finally learnt some healthy self-respect.'

Don had been staring through the windscreen as he spoke. Carolyn turned his troubled face toward her own and pressed her lips to his.

'I love you so much, Don. I promise I'll always be kind to you.'

He smiled, kissed her hand and started the car again.

'It's getting late and I'm hungry,' Don said. 'I've got something in mind for tea. Let's go.'

They quietly drove down the hills as a soft pink sunset appeared in the western sky. They were travelling toward the sea. With Don's revelation still in their thoughts, they started to discuss the welfare of children. To their great surprise, they discovered that they both financially supported the same child protection charity.

Arriving at the beach, Don parked outside a row of little shops. He got out of the car and opened Carolyn's door, helping her out like the gentleman he was. They stood together by the car as Don pointed toward the farthest shopfront.

'I was going to take you to that quiet little café over there. It's a favourite of mine, but I wouldn't mind some fish and chips, actually. What do you feel like?'

'I'm hungry too. I'd like a piece of fish and a pineapple fritter, please. If you pass me that rug on the backseat, I'll find us a place on the beach where we can eat. Oh! And only a couple of chips for me, thanks. I want to fit into my beautiful dress next weekend!'

Whistling an upbeat version of the wedding march, Don reached into the backseat, handed over the rug, and lovingly stroked his fiancée's cheek. Still whistling, he strolled across to the fish shop.

His bride-to-be started walking toward the secluded beach. Passing Don's favourite café, she smiled and waved to the girl who'd served her that morning. After walking down some wooden steps, Carolyn spread out the rug on a few tufts of grass and kicked off her sandals. The fading dusky pink sunset drew her towards the water. With a step as light as her heart, she ran across the wet sand, straight into the foamy tide, and danced around in the shallows like a water sprite.

Pausing for breath, Carolyn reached into the pocket of her dampened floral dress. She drew out the seven folded pages, and tore them into little pieces. As she threw the fragments up in the air, the evening breeze carried them aloft, scattering them like confetti.

Magazine Man

It's never easy starting work in a new city job, just out of school. I was sixteen, timid, not very attractive, and trying hard to learn the ropes. I was amazed to have landed a junior position at a small advertising agency, which produced newspaper advertisements for retailers. In those days, some clients liked hand-drawn illustrations. My role was to learn how to do some of the smaller, less challenging drawings, leaving the elite fashion adverts to the senior artists.

Some experienced staff forgot to lower their voices while criticising my first morning's performance behind my back.

'Do you think she's ever been to an art class?'

'Her shading's much too heavy for newspapers.'

'Can you believe she was the best applicant?'

'Slow as a wet week. She'll never cope with the pressure around here.'

There was nobody available to guide me, as the other artists were frantically working on a big promotion. There was not one word of assistance or encouragement all morning.

At one o'clock, I escaped downstairs to the main street shops. I felt out of place. My mother had sewn me a new outfit, but it was easy to see that other girls' clothes were very different from mine. My father had given me a little money for my first fortnight's expenses, so I bought a sandwich and orange juice, planning to eat in a park around the corner.

The next thing I knew, there were tears in my eyes as I recalled the morning's nasty comments. Embarrassed, I lowered my head, quickly picked up a magazine from a small portable news stand near the gutter and flicked through it. I had no idea that they were allowed to sell magazines featuring girls in birthday suits right where little children could see them!

A slight older man with a refined English accent appeared from behind the stand, asking if I'd like some help.

I looked up, wiping my eyes, as I swiftly replaced the rubbishy magazine. It certainly was different from the *Women's Weekly* my mother bought each week!

'I'm just looking, thanks,' I blurted out.

'That's quite alright, Ma'am,' he said, looking at me through his thick glasses. 'But may I direct you to these more wholesome magazines over here? I'm required to carry some lesser publications that I never recommend to ladies such as yourself, or to true gentlemen, either, for that matter!'

Blushing, I shyly thanked him for his help.

Glancing at my still-damp cheeks, he gently said, 'And I do sincerely wish you a most pleasant afternoon.'

I said something polite in return, hastily squandered money on a gardening magazine for my mother, and took my leave.

I soon found a corner of the nearby park where I could soak up the summer sunshine and pretty scenery. Pondering what had just happened, I recalled the man's appearance. Smartly pressed business shirt and trousers, skilfully-knotted tie, and shiny cufflinks engraved with the letter 'G'. And such flawless speech! My tears ceased as soon as he'd started to speak. He intrigued me. All I knew was I now felt so much better because of him.

The afternoon was not so bad. There were still a couple of snide remarks and sighs, but I didn't let it bother me quite as much. The manager who'd conducted my first interview dropped in to speak to me. Within earshot of those around me, he said how impressed he'd

'May I direct you to these magazines?'

been after looking through my artwork folio at the interview.

'I expect you'll soon be making a real contribution,' he added.

Again, I blushed, but this time with pleasure. He leaned across my desk, shook my hand, and wished me well. After hearing this, the staff started to treat me better, and some friendships started to develop soon after.

There were no more tears.

I soon found my niche, and was surprised to be promoted in quite a short time. I still needed to get out into the fresh air at lunchtimes, so I only went to the staffroom with workmates for tea breaks.

I continued to buy from the magazine seller and looked forward to hearing his polite speech – especially after working each morning with a number of people whose language and manners left a lot to be desired!

My timidity lessened. During lunch breaks I had no trouble in having a quick chat with people behind the counters in various shops (only if they were not too busy, of course). They told me a little about their lives and seemed to enjoy a few words and a laugh. However, my interaction with the old magazine man never went beyond discussing the publications. Somehow, it seemed too familiar to ask personal questions, so I took my cue from him.

In response to his 'Ma'am', I addressed him as 'Sir'. He seemed pleased by that.

I often wondered about his life and thought of all kinds of scenarios. His humble business seemed at odds with his formal, beautiful use of the English language and his polished appearance. He did, however, find giving change somewhat difficult at times. The lenses in his glasses were quite thick, though, so perhaps he simply couldn't see the coins very well.

And then there was the small sepia photo that was hanging at the side of his stand. I worked up the courage to comment about it one day. It was the only time I mentioned anything personal.

'That beautiful lady has such kind eyes, don't you think?'

He nodded. Then, in a faltering voice, he murmured, 'If only … her kindness had been extended to …' He stopped, then added, 'No. Please, excuse me. I won't say a word against her.'

And there he left it. I apologised and never mentioned the subject again. A sweetheart? His wife? His mother? A daughter? I never found out.

A few weeks later, his magazine stand was taken over by a teenage boy. He told me he'd heard that the old man had collapsed right there in the gutter. An ambulance was called, but it was too late.

I privately mourned my friend, despite knowing so little about him. On the days I had seen him, I always felt uplifted. In him, I saw a wonderful blend of humility and dignity. Without him knowing, he taught me how to carry out my work to the very best of my ability, no matter how menial the task.

I missed his courtesy, his sincerity and kindness. I especially missed how he made me, a shy teenager from the wrong side of the tracks, feel worthy of being treated as a lady. I loved to call him 'Sir.'

And the 'G' on his cufflinks? Why, of course it stood for 'Gentleman.'

Testing Times

Circa 1930

Mr Woods, the Grade Six teacher, had never had a moment's worry with Ellie Stirling. She was a bright and obedient student, with an interest in all subjects except arithmetic but, even in that, she succeeded through sheer hard work. She shone on the hockey field, darting between the bigger girls and hitting the ball with great force, despite her short stature! In sewing class she produced delicate embroidered linen which won prizes in their small rural show.

One afternoon, as his students were packing up to go home, Mr Woods called her aside.

'What are you going to do when you leave Primary School, Ellie?' he asked. The final School Certificate tests were looming, and the topic of graduation had just been discussed in class.

'I think I might like to be a schoolteacher like you, Mr Woods. I've started teaching the littlies at Sunday School and I just love it.'

Her teacher paused, knowing that the road ahead would not be easy.

'Well, I'm sure you have the ability, but are you prepared to put in some hard work? It would mean going to High School first and then to a Teachers' College for training. It would be a long time before you could teach in your own classroom.'

'Well, if that's what schoolteachers have to do, then I'll do it too!' she cheerfully replied, swiftly packing her schoolbag before the long walk home.

Later, at teatime, a very happy little twelve-year-old announced to her mother that she'd made up her mind about what she would do when she grew up – she'd like to be a schoolteacher.

***

In their little country town, hardly any grade six girls went on to High School. Most stayed at home, helping their mothers with domestic duties as training for marriage. Others helped out on their parents' farms or, if the work was available, might become a shop assistant or office worker. Secondary schooling for girls was uncommon, and university or other tertiary education was hardly ever considered.

Mr Woods had been thinking about Ellie and her matter-of-fact, easy-going attitude towards entering the teaching profession. Even though she was only a child, he felt that she needed to hear a few cautionary words from her teacher.

The next day on yard duty in the quadrangle, he noticed Ellie sitting alone, biting into an apple. Her friends had already finished their lunches and gone off to play. He strolled over to the wooden seat, and sat at the opposite end.

'Ellie, I know that you're still quite young, but I want you to think about a couple of matters before you make up your mind about High School and Teachers' College.'

His pupil listened carefully. She liked the feeling of being spoken to as though she were an adult.

'You're a clever girl and would make a good teacher, and it's a fine profession for unmarried ladies. But you have to think about what would happen if you want to get married. You might teach for a very short time, but after the wedding you'd probably be busy raising half a dozen children or more. You wouldn't want to ask anyone else to look after your babies, would you? You'd have to leave teaching to care for them. Your training could all be a waste of time.'

Ellie was dumbfounded. Nobody had told her any of *that* before! Of course she wanted to get married one day. But she wanted to be a schoolteacher, too! Trembling with rage, her blue eyes flashed as she jumped up, hurling her uneaten apple into a metal bin.

'Well, I don't care!' she stubbornly bellowed at her shocked teacher. 'I want to be a schoolteacher, so I'm going to find a way somehow.'

With his words of discouragement echoing in her head, she ran into some bushes and sobbed. She'd never reacted so passionately to anything else in her whole life. To her credit, after lunchtime she apologised, hardly daring to look her favourite teacher in the eye.

'I'm sorry I yelled at you, Mr Woods. It's just that I want to be a teacher too, and it's not fair.'

He gently told her that he understood how she felt about teaching and accepted her apology. Ellie promised that she would never lose her temper or speak to any teacher in that way again. They agreed that the incident shouldn't be discussed any further, which was a great relief to Ellie. She certainly wouldn't be telling her mother about it!

***

After lessons had finished one afternoon, Ellie's mother knocked on the door of Mr Woods' classroom. She was hoping for a meeting with Mr Woods, which he duly granted. Ellie, fortunately, was playing hockey, so didn't know her mother was there. Mrs Stirling's deportment, well-tailored dress and tone of voice were those of a cultured lady. After politely greeting the teacher, she didn't waste any time.

'Sir, I'm here about a delicate matter, which must remain private, if you please. I have a request. Ellie recently mentioned the requirements regarding a teaching career and, as a result, I told her that if she can achieve dux of Grade Six, I'll pay for her to go to High School. I want her to keep striving, you see. The problem is that after making inquiries on the telephone today, I've found that I simply cannot afford the fees for a Secondary School, and certainly not those for a Teachers' College!'

The teacher scratched his head, puzzled. He knew Mrs Stirling had a job, because he bought delicious vanilla slices from the bakery where she worked. Two incomes in one family would keep the wolf from the door in any normal rural household. He studied her expressive face as she raised her chin a little higher, unconsciously trying to project an air of dignity. If she was feeling humiliated, it didn't show. Mr Woods wondered where this was leading, but signalled with an outstretched hand for the lady to continue.

'I can see you find that hard to believe, sir, but the truth is that my husband is not a good provider, and is rarely at home. He's employed as a drover, you see, but there's little for the men to do in the evenings except drink in hotels. I'm afraid that's where all his money goes. I've trusted very few people around here with that confidential information. I hope you will honour that confidence, too.'

'Of course, Mrs Stirling. But you mentioned a request?'

She straightened her shoulders further and took a deep breath. It was obvious to the teacher that there was something even more difficult to be said. He admired her composure and gave her a smile of encouragement to continue.

'I'm very reluctant to ask this, but I was wondering if you could ensure that Ellie will *not* achieve dux of the school. She's shown that she's capable of it, but second or third place would get me out of this embarrassing difficulty. I know Ellie will succeed in whatever she undertakes in life. I'm afraid it simply can't be school teaching.'

Mr Woods hadn't been expecting that! He was not a heartless man. He knew that Ellie's mother would have put a lot of thought into what she was asking, but what could he do? He told her that he understood her reason, but changing even one mark was something that he could not, in all conscience, bring himself to do, either professionally or personally.

'I'm truly sorry, Mrs Stirling, but that would be unethical. I do wish you well, though. We'll simply have to hope that combining my marks with those of the other teachers will bring about the result that you need.'

She thanked the teacher for his time and left the room. It was only then that she dropped her guard, pain written all over her face.

***

A couple of weeks later, Ellie stayed behind after the last class in order to ask a favour of Mr Woods. Her behaviour had been impeccable since their last serious talk, so she hoped he'd be willing to help her. Her teacher was standing at the blackboard, writing up notes for the next day's history lesson. Turning to speak, he could see that her usually alert eyes were a little downcast. She seemed worried. He put down the chalk, drew up a chair next to his desk, and gave her his full attention.

'Tell me what's on your mind, young lady,' he coaxed, trying to allay her anxiety with a kind tone.

'Mr Woods, can you please help me? My mum's got a job at the bakery, but lately she's been working too hard. She's getting up at four o'clock in the morning to light the ovens at five, and she has to keep going all day. She's awfully tired, all the time. And it's my fault. I think she's saving up so I can go to High School. She told me she'd pay for me go if I get the top marks in Grade Six.'

'Hmm. I can understand your worry, Ellie, but you need to go to High School and Teachers' College if you're going to be a schoolteacher. Perhaps your mother is willing to work long hours if she can help make that happen. But I can't see how I can help.'

'But you can, Mr Woods. It's easy! And Mum would never have to know about it. Can you just make sure I *don't* get top marks in the tests this year? I'd even be happy with fifty-one percent, as long as it's not a hundred percent, or whatever the best mark is.'

Her teacher looked steadily into Ellie's eyes, shaking his head sadly. Her unselfish concern for her mother had touched his heart deeply, but he couldn't show it.

'No, Ellie. I'm sorry. I'd very much like to help you, but teachers have to be honest and fair at all times, especially when marking tests. There's no room for dishonesty, whatever the reason. Now don't you forget that; and don't you try doing any less than your best in the tests, because I'll know!' he said, in a mildly threatening tone.

Ellie lowered her head, slinging her schoolbag over her drooping shoulders, and made her way towards the door without speaking. She didn't even say 'thank you' or 'goodbye.' Deeply in thought, she'd completely forgotten her manners. She left the classroom, crestfallen.

****

The night following the completion of the year's testing, Mr Woods settled down at his kitchen table to begin reading and marking the students' papers. His approach was orderly, well-practiced, and time-consuming. As with other years, it took him two weekends to complete. Along with his own markings, he also had to add the physical education and sewing teachers' scores. This total gave him each pupil's final position in the class.

Not surprisingly, Ellie did very well in his own subjects, but the teacher's heart sank as he realised that a perfect result for needlework had contributed towards Ellie achieving the Grade Six top score of ninety-eight percent. Despairing, he couldn't bring himself to write it on her report.

The ink dried on the pen as he pondered Mrs Stirling's and Ellie's pleas, along with his own replies. He had spoken to each one about integrity. He could not backtrack, as he knew

Mr Woods' approach was orderly.

that if the subject was raised again by either mother or daughter, he had to be able to look them in the eye. So, he reluctantly dipped the nib of the pen in the ink-well and wrote down 'ninety-eight' on the report.

Mr Woods reflected on the probable outcome of his action. He knew he could not change it now. Was there ever a case for dropping his high standards?

Perhaps there was. He picked up the report of the child who had scored ninety-seven, and quickly and deliberately wrote down 'ninety-nine percent.'

Author's note …

Although the story you've just read is fiction, it was inspired by my mother's experience. Lacking opportunity in her youth, and with great determination, she finally fulfilled her heartfelt desire to become a teacher, at the age of thirty-five.

I like to think that 'Ellie' also eventually achieved her ambition, don't you?

It Started in the Sixties

I wasn't like the other admiring fans at the stage door, after the Gregg Owens concert. I didn't want anything from him. No autograph, no photo, no invitation to a party. I just stood a bit further down the hallway and observed the way he related to people. He certainly had the outward charms of a pop singer, with his blonde hair, pale blue satin jacket and an easy-going manner. Despite these, he seemed genuinely interested in each person, giving them his time and full attention. He even grinned at me from a distance and beckoned for me to join them. Not wanting special attention, I shook my head and retreated.

It was 1965. Gregg was only eighteen, but had already put his own stamp on music that appealed to sixteen-year-olds like me, with his light-hearted pop songs and soulful ballads. He behaved well in public, speaking respectfully to young and old alike. This impressed my parents and, consequently, Mum bought me a ticket to Gregg's concert at the local Town Hall. I was happy to go alone, seated quite close to the stage in a central aisle seat.

Gregg's warm voice could be gentle, bright or booming, as each song demanded. There were some wonderful arrangements that gave his sound real originality. In the short breaks between brackets, he and his backing group entertained us with their banter, but when he started to sing my favourite love song, I could only focus on him. He seemed to be looking right at me, singing my thoughts. I was totally entranced! I never could have screamed like the girls around me. How could they spoil the moment, the reflective music, with such awful noise?

Afterwards, Mum waited for me at the top of the Town Hall steps. Childhood poliomyelitis had left me in need of forearm crutches, so she wanted to make sure I could manage the scores of steps leading down to the footpath. The wheelchair that I sometimes used would have been helpful if a different entry point to the auditorium could be found, but wheelchair access could not be guaranteed. Anyway, I didn't want to stand out in the crowd, and I certainly didn't want to be seen as someone to be handled with kid gloves. With crutches only, I felt more like everyone else.

As Mum started the drive home, I thanked her for booking a seat with such a good view of the stage. For the rest of the trip, I couldn't stop talking about Gregg and his music. She could tell I was still up in the clouds.

'Well, why don't you arrange to interview him for your school magazine?' she suggested.

'Mum! Don't you know how hard that'd be?' I wailed. 'He's really going somewhere! He's been on TV already and he's going to do two interstate concerts soon. I wouldn't stand a chance.'

'Nothing ventured, nothing gained,' she chanted. 'Remember how you thought your college application would never be accepted? Look at you now! You're on the magazine committee, and writing some impressive articles.'

My parents were both known for their persistence, so a defeatist attitude was never tolerated at home. I set to work and within a fortnight had succeeded in my quest. Gaining Gregg's permission for an interview was relatively easy, but obtaining the support of Mr Stoner, the college Headmaster, was much more difficult. However, his permission was eventually given, and my excitement knew no bounds. Mr Stoner insisted I should use my wheelchair in case 'the visitor' wanted a tour of the school. I could see that walking with crutches might slow us down a little if that occurred.

It wasn't long before I was seated in a private room, awaiting Gregg's arrival. Right on time, he arrived, was introduced, and sat facing me. Trembling slightly, I found myself looking straight into my favourite singer's searching eyes. His Old Spice aftershave wafted toward me. With my notebook in hand and pen poised, I nervously thanked him for coming in for the interview.

Mr Stoner watched us through the open adjoining door to his office as I went through all my carefully-prepared notes, trying not to ask tedious questions. It was hard to relax and be natural, knowing that every word could be heard by the Headmaster. I even found myself wondering what Mr Stoner thought when Gregg said he'd hated school and left to start work as soon as he'd turned fifteen. I soon learnt the answer after the interview, as we were about to say our farewells.

'Err, Mr Owens,' Mr Stoner said, frowning. 'I need to say that the magazine article will be edited by me for content. I'm sure this student's writing standard will be excellent, but I won't include your educational history. I'd prefer the tone of the story to be more ... err ... *aspirational* for our students here. I'm sure you understand.'

'I certainly do!' replied Gregg, grimly. He ignored Mr Stoner's outstretched hand, thanked me, and walked away.

Alarmed, I released the brake of my chair and rolled toward the door as fast as I could. Seeing Gregg in the distance, I whizzed across the schoolyard.

'Gregg!' I called out. He turned around, anger etched across his face. I caught up with him just before he reached the school gate. 'I'm sorry. After you came from over the other side of town just for us, to treat you like that was horrible. If he doesn't like what I write, I'll rip it up right under his nose, and stuff the paper down his big mouth!'

I watched Gregg's facial expression as it changed to a wide grin. Finally, he threw back his head and laughed. 'Now, what would be the use of that? Nobody would get to read it!'

Appreciating his good humour, I laughed too. 'Well, maybe my idea isn't very wise. But listen, I've got an old typewriter at home, so I'll tap out the article there without anyone breathing down my neck. I'll post it to you and keep some carbon-paper copies for the editing. At least that way you'll see the original version. Where would you like me to send it?'

Gregg fossicked in his pockets for pen and paper without success, so I offered him mine.

He found a seat under a droopy peppercorn tree. We exchanged details and had a short but memorable conversation, during which he asked me about my family, my interests and future ambitions. Then he sensitively asked about the reason for the wheelchair. I told him that I'd been part of the '52 polio epidemic when I was three, but added that I walked quite well with forearm crutches.

'I've seen you before, haven't I?' he asked. His hazel eyes widened, along with his smile. 'You were at my last concert. You came backstage, but you wouldn't come over for a chat. I wanted to talk to you, but by the time I was free you'd gone.'

I sheepishly confessed that he was right, blaming self-consciousness. I was secretly flattered that he'd remembered me.

A scowling Mr Stoner appeared and firmly beckoned me back to class.

'See ya next time,' Gregg whispered, and with that, the singer was gone.

I didn't discuss a word of our conversation with anyone at school. That time alone with Gregg was too precious to share.

I was so angry about the Headmaster's comments that the magazine article almost wrote itself. I reported my questions and all of Gregg's answers, including his minimal years at school, but turned the following last two paragraphs into a challenge for the students:

Yes, Gregg Owens did leave his neglected little school at a young age, but look at what he's already accomplished in only three years. He works in retailing during the day, and has made his own way into the music industry, building a singing career at night and on weekends with very little assistance. This hard work has led Gregg into negotiating a recording contract. He has attained all of this through his own efforts. In the near future, he plans to use his talents to raise money for charity and other worthwhile causes. All this and he's only eighteen.

Conversely, some of us expect others to open doors to our future. We've become used to a privileged education, where opportunities are laid at our feet, and we take it all for granted. So I ask this question: are we going to waste the wonderful opportunities that our college offers, or work towards our future goals with our utmost effort?

Surprisingly, the article was published with no omissions. I mailed a copy of the magazine to Gregg. He was impressed. After that, I audaciously offered to try out as his press publicist in my spare time, just for fun. Gregg took me seriously. He liked my work and believed in me. He even insisted on paying the going rate.

Gregg also encouraged me to think about making freelance writing my career. Upon leaving school two years later, I did just that.

There seemed to be limitless topics to write about. I urged people to join me in tackling unkind or unjust practices, and to speak up for the powerless. Some readers, who also wanted to achieve change for the better, sent wonderful letters of support. They left me feeling that I was doing something worthwhile.

Not surprisingly, one issue that I raised was the provision of wheelchair access in public buildings, especially in toilet areas. In another article, I stressed the need for all parents to ensure that their children be given the anti-polio Sabin vaccine.

***

As the sixties rolled into the seventies, there were so many other matters to write about: the white Australia policy, the abduction of indigenous children, 'no-fault' divorce, the Vietnam War, acceptance of same-sex relationships, the welfare of children and adults in institutions, and the long-awaited equal pay for women, to name some.

Along with those efforts, I still wrote a lot of promotional material for Gregg on a regular basis, as he'd become even more popular over time. His LP records sold fast and he was on the road quite often. Whenever he flew home between concert tours, we'd work together, tossing around ideas for promoting good causes. We had a lot of laughs during those sessions, but most importantly, we achieved some excellent outcomes for those who would benefit from Gregg's generosity.

In February each year, Gregg took a month off to unwind, relax in his spacious home and catch up with friends. On one such occasion, he took me aside and confided something that took me by surprise.

'I've got something to tell you, and I want you to hear it from me first. You know Joanne, don't you?' he asked. 'She's that nice young lady who comes in to do the bookkeeping on Fridays. Well, we've been seeing a fair bit of each other, and last night I popped the question. She said yes. We're planning to get married in about six months. What do you think?'

To say I was taken aback was an understatement. Gregg had dated some lovely women in the past, but it never went beyond that. What could I do other than be happy for him? Recovering quickly, I immediately told him so, injecting some excitement into my voice. I liked Joanne, and could understand why Gregg had fallen for her.

The romantic feelings that had overwhelmed me as a teenager had long since been put aside in favour of our good working relationship. Anyway, I could never confess my true feelings now that he was about to be married. I just felt privileged to be able to work with such an admirable man, and to be known as one of his closest friends.

The announcement of the approaching wedding was made, but the public's curiosity about Joanne was unforeseen. The constant attention from Gregg's fans and some journalists of the lowest kind made her life unbearable. Hurtful stories were written about the sweet young woman, with no basis at all. Gregg spoke up for her against the defamation, but the damage was done. Sadly, Joanne called off the engagement. I felt genuinely sorry for them both, as they had seemed very happy together.

The broken engagement coincided with Gregg's thirtieth birthday, and he didn't want any celebration. It was months before he was able to face the public again. Even when it was time to get back to work, he couldn't summon the energy to go back on the road, so the exhausting national tours ceased. He limited his live performances to the occasional small concert in the state's regional areas. Gregg was surprised at how much he enjoyed them, and resolved to weave those venues into his normal schedule. He continued recording in the privacy of his home studio.

Of course, I tried to be a loyal and supportive friend to him during that time. It took three years before Gregg's life returned to normal, albeit at a slightly slower pace. It almost seemed as though he'd been waiting for the seventies to pass, so that he could start the new decade afresh. He even threw an extravagant belated thirtieth birthday party on the first of January, 1980. It didn't seem to bother anyone that he was actually thirty-three years old by then! All we cared about was that our old Gregg was back.

***

I was planning to move out of my tiny flat and, in passing, mentioned my decision to Gregg. Pondering for a minute or two, he had an idea: I could move into the granny flat built onto the side of his home. The previous owners had originally built it for their elderly mother.

Despite her physical disability, she still wanted her own independence, so they reached a compromise by building the granny flat. It also allowed the grandkids to visit her whenever they wanted. Gregg explained that after he bought the house, he'd just used the space for storage. I'd never known of the flat's existence, having previously been only in the main part of the house.

'What do you think? Would you consider it?' he asked.

'This is a great idea,' I replied. 'Considering how often we need to consult for work.'

Gregg didn't want to show me the flat straight away. It needed to be cleared out and cleaned up first.

'Give me a month,' he said. 'Then you can inspect it.'

Exactly thirty days later, I was at the familiar address, perched in my wheelchair, trying out the flat's accessibility. It had a shallow ramp to the wide entrance door, so we were off to a good start.

Sounding like a real estate agent, Gregg pointed out features that he knew would interest me, as I craned my head to see what was around each corner.

'This is the main living area here, but it's more like a studio-style bedsitter, with loads more space. The bench in the kitchenette over there's at standing level, but it steps down to sitting level, too, with room for a wheelchair underneath. Come and see the bathroom. It's huge! There's an intercom to the main house, and grab-rails everywhere, too. Have a good look around, then tell me what you think.'

I'd said nothing, but had taken in everything. Besides all the practical features, I loved the light, bright atmosphere of the place. With its steeply sloping ceiling and row of skylight windows, it reminded me of how an alpine chalet might look. There was a big window at floor level that opened out to a private courtyard, too.

'It's perfect, Gregg,' I declared. 'There's not a thing I would change. How long before I can move in?'

'Hang on,' he cautioned. 'We're not through yet.' He grinned mischievously. I watched him roll back a wide sliding door to reveal a roomy, well-lit study area, equipped with new office furniture. Gregg's larger study and office were through a doorway at one end. It was the ideal workspace for writing alone or working together.

'Gregg, did you set up this writing room for me?' I asked incredulously. Quietly, he simply said that I'd already paid for it many times over, and that he wanted to thank me for always being there for him, especially after the broken engagement. He'd ordered a nice big computer for me too, as he'd heard that all the writers were using them. Forever grateful for his thoughtfulness, I moved in a fortnight later. He would only accept a very modest sum for the rent.

The convenience of living and working in one place made life a whole lot easier. Gregg respected the privacy of my living space and always knocked before entering the writing room.

I could never repay his kindness, but attempted to do so by working even harder.

When working on publicity, we put in long hours but I didn't mind if it meant needy people or organisations would benefit from Gregg's involvement. He regularly recorded new material, and during television and radio interviews that preceded their release, he used his celebrity status to promote his favourite charities.

Some fans couldn't see past his good looks, and assumed that he paid others to do all the thinking for him. Gregg followed his own path, used his own instincts. Smart investment of his earnings early in his career meant he became quite wealthy, but never selfish. With his big, generous heart, philanthropy had always been his motivation.

I could never understand why he and I got along so well and were able to work together so successfully. He was different from me – a real people person. By nature, he was gregarious and at ease in the sparkling entertainment world. I, however, preferred my own cosy environment, but Gregg could be very persuasive. Now and then I'd go along to one of his industry's big events. He always made a fuss of me when I was dressed up and ready to leave for the venue.

'Look at you!' he'd exclaim. 'I know who's the photogenic one around here, and it's not me!'

With that kind of encouragement, my confidence grew and I learnt to enjoy his special occasions.

At home, in my leisure time, I'd taken up the composition of words to his new tunes, and Gregg flattered me by using most of them. Come to think of it, that creative outlet probably made me a part of the entertainment world, after all!

***

I'd been living in my new home for a couple of years when an office assistant unknowingly let a cat out of the bag. I'd been talking to her about my flat, but what she said in response didn't make any sense to me. Gregg overheard. He beckoned me into his office and shut the door.

'There was never any disabled granny in the granny flat,' he admitted, his face reddening as he sheepishly explained. 'In fact, there was never any granny flat at all! Originally, there was just one big empty room attached to the house – more like a wing, really. I had it blocked off, except for the connecting office door.'

Dumbfounded, I let him continue.

'I had fun drawing up a plan for the renovators. They fitted out the whole flat in a month – the kitchenette, the bathroom, the grab rails, even the ramp at the front door! I designed every last detail with you in mind, in the hope that some feature or other might persuade you to live here.'

Astounded, I couldn't believe what I was

hearing. Gregg was known for his honesty, but that spur-of-the-moment story had been one big, fat, beautiful lie!

'Why would you go to all that trouble before I'd even seen it?' I asked. 'What if I didn't like it?'

'I was willing to take that risk,' he answered. 'I would've rented it out to someone else if you didn't want it. It was just that I liked the idea of having you around, so I tried to make the flat something that you couldn't resist.'

His words, *I liked the idea of having you around,* resonated in my head for ages. I told myself I was reading too much into them.

***

Thus another decade ticked over, bringing us into the nineties. By 1990, Gregg and I had both turned forty, fairly uneventfully. Big parties had given way to nice restaurant meals with family and friends. He was mellowing a little and I liked the change of pace.

I suppose we were so busy with our projects, secure in our satisfying working relationship, that we weren't aware of what others could see. My deep feelings for Gregg had remained hidden since our first meeting. I'd often wondered if he ever felt a similar attraction toward me. If so, he had never told me. Yet, there must have been something about the way we related that caused other people to wonder if we were a couple … a gay couple. Some of our friends were in no doubt. They had made that assumption long before Gregg was brave enough to reveal to me where his heart really lay.

So, after twenty-five years as simply colleagues and good friends, we at last confessed our profound love to each other. The mutual attraction had been there right from the start, but Gregg had battled his private yearnings, as had I.

For us, the open, honest recognition of our feelings and subsequent total commitment to each other was breathtaking.

***

These days, our longed-for life together really does get better with every passing year. Now in his late sixties, Gregg's voice is still strong enough to record, with only a little tweaking by the technicians if needed. He still has a huge following.

Despite moving around quite well on crutches, I do experience some of the muscle weakness and fatigue associated with post-polio syndrome. As I get older, I find it more comfortable to use a wheelchair to combat this.

Gregg's gentle care for me when I'm having a bad day is a blessing that I never take for granted.

He truly is the love of my life.

Labours of Love

Rock ... rock ... rock.

The precious newborn baby in my arms yawns, trembles a little, and closes his puffy eyelids, as I softly sing to the rocking chair's rhythm. The nurse has only told me his first name, but that's the case with all of the babies in this corner of the nursery. A small team of volunteers like me give additional care until they're ready to go home from the hospital.

Quiet talking, singing, and moving around are meant to stimulate the baby's level of alertness and, indeed, that approach brings the desired result. But there's a time to be calm too.

I return him to his cot for a gentle back rub, as he settles for a short sleep before bottle time. Sitting next to him, I silently take in a little of what's happening around me. I love the atmosphere of this place.

Next to my small alcove are rows of mostly occupied tiny cots. In an adjoining section, from a distance, I can see the ICU cribs. Each crib has a fragile little baby within its transparent walls, along with the usual tubes and equipment. Anxious parents keep vigil if they can, or visit as often as possible. Later, it's lovely to see them start to relax and grow in confidence as their baby's condition improves.

Unfortunately, this is not always the case.

This ward is a familiar place; I've been coming here for quite a few years now. It became even more familiar when my sister, Trish, after a series of miscarriages, had a premature little girl who was rushed here with breathing problems. The baby didn't survive despite weeks of skilled care. Later, there was another miscarriage, then twin boys who had to be delivered early. One died at birth, and the other lasted only a few hours.

Trish and her husband, Matt, were devastated. Family and friends tried to be as supportive as possible, but there was little we could do or say to relieve their pain. The heartbroken couple was in a dark valley that only they could traverse.

***

A couple of months after their latest tragedy, Trish dropped around to my house for one of our morning chats, but this time, she carried a suitcase. I held my breath, expecting the worst. Marriages sometimes falter under the strain and grief of losing *one* child, let alone several. I knew that Matt had been very caring, but he'd become much quieter as he struggled to make sense of yet another heartbreak.

'Trish, what's happened?' I asked, wrapping my arms around her. 'Are you alright? Is Matt okay?'

'Most days we manage, some better than others. But what were you expecting? Oh! The case! No, Kerrie. It's nothing like that. I just want my big sister to see what's in it, but later on will do,' she said, leaving the case in the hallway.

Trish found her favourite bar stool at the kitchen bench while I set about making two big mugs of frothy cappuccino. From the pantry I produced her favourite nut loaf and sliced it thickly, knowing that she liked it that way.

'I'll spread the butter,' she offered, and once that task was completed, we carried the coffee and cake to the big kitchen table and settled in for a chin-wag.

I studied her face for a moment, and decided that her most recent bereavement had taken its toll. It seemed as though the light in her once-bright eyes had dimmed. I sipped my hot coffee, and asked a simple question. 'How are you *really*, Trish?'

'I'm not terribly good, actually,' she replied.

'I'm here because I want to tell you something.'

'Oh no,' I said, greatly concerned. 'What's been going on?'

Trish gave a sigh, and explained.

'Well, Matt and I were considering trying for another baby, but it's just not going to happen. Neither of us think we can handle the possibility of another loss. Anyway, we talked to my specialist last week, and he doesn't want to see me go through another pregnancy. He said it would be too risky now, so the final decision's been made.'

'Oh, Trish. What can I say?' was all I could manage. Seeking the comfort of her big sister's arms, Trish leaned in towards me. I wrapped her in my embrace as, together, we wept for the dream that was not to be.

It was some time before we found our voices again. I topped up the coffees and picked up where we'd left off.

'You've been through so much, Trish,' I said, 'but there are other options. I assume you and Matt have looked at adoption?'

'We made enquiries, but it's such a lengthy process these days, and it's not always smooth sailing. We're emotionally wrung out, Kerrie, and we aren't getting any younger, you know. We'll be *forty* soon! We don't want to be on walking frames for our child's first day of school.'

We both laughed at that absurd picture, despite the sadness of the decision that she and Matt had made together. I could see that age wasn't the real issue here. Besides, there are many first-time parents in their forties and even fifties these days. No, it seemed to me that they just needed time for their broken hearts to heal. More than anything else, they needed each other.

***

Trish and I were clearing away the morning tea dishes when I remembered the suitcase in the hallway.

'Are you going to show me what's in it now?' I asked, curious to know of the contents.

'Yes, I just need you to help me lift it on to the table.'

Together, we carefully placed the case within easy reach. Trish opened the lid and lifted the pastel paper covering. She handed me a soft little item, enclosed in a thin piece of tissue paper. I gently pulled back the tissue to find a small pale blue beanie, embroidered with lemon ducklings. It was perfectly made. I reverently handed it back to her, not daring to speak, in case I broke down. It was only the first of many exquisite items of baby clothing. These were the tiny garments that I had watched her knit during each pregnancy, but there were even more than I remembered. There'd been so much anticipation, so much care, and so much love that had gone into every dainty stitch.

We both became teary, as we tenderly handled each item. There were precious little jackets, jumpers, dresses, pantsuits, rompers, overalls, beanies, bonnets and bootees. Small soft toys filled the spaces. In fact, it seemed that anything that could be knitted for babies was in this suitcase. We replaced them all, and closed the lid.

'Why are you showing them to me now?' I asked. 'Do you want me to save them for our grandchildren?'

Trish dabbed her eyes and tilted her chin resolutely.

'Sorry, Kerrie. No. I'd like them to go to your special care nursery at the hospital. When I used to visit our babies, I noticed that some of the mothers don't dress their little ones in particularly special outfits when they go home for the first time. Maybe they can't afford it, or don't have anyone in their lives who can make them.'

'That's such a beautiful idea,' I said quietly. 'It's just like you to give away something that you treasure so much. My little sister's got a very big heart.'

Smiling, Trish turned to me and we hugged again. She was ready to go home. I promised to carry out her wishes by delivering the case of baby clothes to the hospital.

'Thank you, Kerrie,' she whispered. Standing next to the suitcase, she caressed the closed lid, planted a soft kiss on it, and left.

***

At the hospital, the idea of starting a collection was well received. After a while, volunteer knitters for the Auxiliary Shop said they'd like to add to Trish's beautiful gift in an ongoing way. Soon, every one of the 'special' babies that our team cared for was sent home with at least one little outfit, sometimes more, depending on the circumstances. Now and then, I'd take a thank you note from a grateful mother to Trish. She was always touched that someone had taken the time to write.

No one knew except my husband what makes the babies in our corner of the nursery particularly special – not even Trish. I had to protect the privacy of the mothers, but felt that my sister now had a right to know something about those who were receiving her handiwork.

I called into her house one windy afternoon, just in time to help bring in the washing before it blew off her line. Back in the kitchen, I folded sheets and towels as Trish started to iron some shirts. Hoping I was doing the right thing, I explained why I was there. She seemed eager to find out more, as I started to fill her in.

'The babies I care for need extra attention because they've been born to drug-addicted mothers.'

Trish covered her mouth with her hand, as I haltingly kept going.

'Their dependence is carried through to their babies, so after they're born, the babies go through withdrawal, and need to be eased off whatever drug has been passed on. They're given medication and specialised nursing, with extra attention and cuddles from people like me.'

I'd been anxiously watching Trish's reaction. Her eyes were blazing with anger, her face flushed. She thumped the ironing board with clenched fists.

'Kerrie! How could a mother do that to her helpless little *baby*?' she cried passionately. 'Couldn't she kick the habit for the sake of her child?'

I set aside the washing basket and turned off the iron from the wall beside my sister.

'Come and sit here with me Trish,' I coaxed.

We sat at the dining table, where I gently stroked her hand in an effort to calm her. Although inwardly rattled, I tried to keep my voice steady as I answered her heartfelt questions.

'Some of the pregnant girls try to stop, or at least want to, but if they go cold turkey, it can have a bad effect on the baby, and she could miscarry. They're advised to go onto methadone for the rest of the pregnancy, because it's better for both of them. It takes a lot of commitment to do that. Honestly, in some ways these girls are no different from you and me.'

'What do you mean?' she asked a little more calmly. 'I find that very hard to believe.'

I tried to sympathetically explain what I'd learnt over the years.

'They really are just like anyone else.' I said. 'Even when the pregnancy's unplanned, they want the best for their babies, and love them as much as any other mother. Their circumstances might be a whole lot different from ours, but who knows what drives a person down that path?'

With her elbows on the table and face cupped in her hands, Trish seemed to be deep in thought. I gave her some time to reflect before continuing.

'They're often victimised women who've been badly treated in a whole range of ways – from childhood onwards in some cases – and they haven't asked for help. Their love for their unborn babies sometimes pushes them to seek help for the first time in their lives. That takes courage.'

'It must be hard to admit there's a problem,' Trish commented. 'I guess you're right about needing courage.' Her first angry reaction had been perfectly understandable, but she seemed to have absorbed what I said, and looked more composed. 'But what happens to the babies if the mothers can't stay off drugs?' she asked.

'Well, the hospital has social workers who keep an eye on things. If the little one can't be properly cared for at home, they go to a temporary foster mother. She prepares the baby for longer-term fostering or even adoption, if that seems to be the best thing for the child. These days, it can sometimes be arranged for the birth mother to have contact with her baby as it grows, so she doesn't have to spend the rest of her life wondering about her child.'

'Oh,' was all that she said.

***

Rock … rock … rock.

The tiny infant falls asleep to the rhythm of the rocking chair that takes pride of place in Trish and Matt's family room. For over twenty years now, Trish has prepared numerous babies for their new families. She loves her role. She's said that, if she has her way, she'll keep on fostering until she has to swap the pram for a walking frame! Then she plans to teach me how to knit, so that we can click-clack away together, knitting for the hospital.

Rock … rock … rock.

The tiny infant falls alseep to the rhythm.

Reflections

How could Mike know that anything of significance was about to occur? It was late in the afternoon, and here he was enjoying a ginger ale while sitting at a small table on the deck of a waterside restaurant.

Feeling a cool spot on the top of his balding head, Mike patted it with his hand.

'Arrgh! Blasted seagulls!' he yelled. Somewhat rattled, he wiped his head and hands with a paper serviette, spreading the mess further.

'I'll get something to help you, mate,' one of the men called from a group at the next table. Mike's gaze followed the younger man as he loped toward the indoor bistro. He noticed a business suit minus its coat, and a loosened tie. Sunglasses and a canvas hat completed the stranger's attempt at a casual look.

'Kel's a take-charge sort of bloke,' someone from the helpful man's table explained. 'He'll have you sorted out in no time.'

Mike felt his face burning and suspected it looked bright red.

Kel soon returned with some moist towelettes.

'You'd better do it for me,' Mike said to him, somewhat embarrassed. 'I can't see a damn thing up there.'

Unconcerned by the edict, Kel wiped the older man's bald spot, along with a couple of strands of hair below it. After both men had cleaned their hands, Kel searched for a bin, then returned to his own table.

'Thanks, mate!' Mike called out. 'You're a champion.'

'No worries, squire!' replied Kel.

Mike liked this restaurant, Reflections. He'd discovered it soon after the start of his Sydney holiday. That was three weeks ago and he was certain that, with one week left, he'd keep coming back – despite the badly-behaved seagull. Appreciating the good food at reasonable prices, Mike saw no need to dine elsewhere. He'd arrive in the late afternoon and eat in solitude, watching the strands of winking lights across the water as dusk set in.

He had a favourite table on the elevated wooden deck. It was right on the promenade of Darling Harbour, along with other restaurants, coffee shops and all kinds of tourist attractions. Visitors and locals alike enjoyed strolling across a magnificent old pedestrian bridge, with some of them pausing to look at the various marine vessels secured in the water below.

Mike had never seen this city before. He was a Melbourne boy through and through, but the beautiful harbour setting really impressed him.

As he waited for his meal, Mike thought about what the last month or two had brought him and where life was going. He'd turned sixty-five in the week that followed his retirement. To celebrate, he was treating himself to a month in Sydney. He thought life was going to be pretty uneventful once this holiday was over.

A large serve of Chicken Caesar arrived. It was just the thing for a warm summer evening. Mike licked his lips, anticipating the contrasting elements of his favourite salad. Just as he picked up his cutlery to dig in to the meal, a shadow flashed across the table. Another seagull swooped, carrying away a large sliver of chicken!

'Get away, you rotten thief!' Mike yelled, waving his knife and fork in the air.

The men around the nearby table tried to suppress their mirth, but Kel jumped up again, concerned for the older man. Just as he stepped across to Mike's table, *another* audacious bird plunged from the sky, stole *more* chicken from Mike's plate, and disappeared above some adjacent buildings!

'What the heck's going on here?' Mike shouted.

'Okay, mate,' said Kel. 'Let's get away from here.' He ushered Mike to a table inside the bistro, after letting his friends know he'd be back later on. 'I'm going to speak to the head waitress.' Kel found her within no time and, turning on the charm, he described the upsetting incidents. The waitress recognised Mike as a daily visitor and arranged for *two* meals 'on the house'. Returning with a triumphant grin and two menus, Kel reported the outcome of his complaint, although he wondered whether he'd be asked to eat at Mike's table.

'Well, it looks as though I've got company,' Mike said, smiling for the first time. 'Be my guest. Well done.'

'Thanks. All part of the service, sir. Do you want a salad again or something else?' Kel asked, handing over a menu. He excused himself, in order to tell his friends what had happened, suggesting they shouldn't wait for him. He returned to Mike's table as the waitress approached to take the orders.

Mike was ready. Shunning the salads, he opted for steak and chips instead, along with a beer.

'Make that two, thanks,' Kel told the waitress.

Properly introducing themselves at last, relaxed conversation flowed as they waited for their meals.

'So,' said Mike, crossing his arms like a footballer in a team photo, 'what makes a fella like you go all out to help an old codger like me?'

Kel shrugged. 'Um, I dunno. I suppose I just get on well with older people. I come from a big family. There were eight of us kids. I was the baby, so I'm used to knocking about with anyone older than me.'

Mike nodded, unfolding his arms.

Kel wasn't finished yet. 'Listen, to be honest, there's another reason besides that. I've been staring at you because you look a bit like me.'

'Well, it's hard for me to tell what you look like, with those damned sunglasses on your nose,' Mike bluntly commented.

'Oh! Sorry, mate. I forgot I was still wearing them.' Kel placed them in his shirt pocket and removed his canvas hat.

With the younger man's features exposed for the first time, Mike suddenly felt as though he was looking in a mirror. He instantly recognised his younger self at around Kel's age – which he guessed was about forty-five. He couldn't stop looking at the coarse sandy thatch, thick eyebrows, very unusual tan-coloured eyes, prominent nose and jawline. Mike used to look *just* like that!

The topic of conversation quickly turned to sport, business, Kel's marriage, and Mike's divorce.

After learning that Mike had been a landscape gardener, Kel proudly showed a photo of his pretty wife and himself, both standing with another woman outside a lovely cottage garden.

After admiring the pastel floral effects, Mike studied the people in the photo. Kel and his wife, Katy, looked relaxed and happy, one each side of the second female figure. Mike focused on this woman's beautiful, unforgettable smile. It was still instantly recognisable despite the passing of over four decades! He was absolutely certain that the little woman in the photo had to be his teenage sweetheart, Mary.

Mike's stomach churned and he almost stopped breathing. He hadn't seen Mary since her family moved away in a hurry, leaving no forwarding address. At the time, he'd wondered if Mary might be pregnant. Was the person in the photo Kel's mother? And if she was, that could mean ...

Mike was shaken up, but tried to sound nonchalant. He said some complimentary words about Katy, then pointed to the other woman in the photo.

'And who's the lady with you and Katy?'

'That's Mary, my big sister,' Kel replied. 'She's the eldest out of the eight of us, and pretty amazing, really. She stayed at home in Goulburn to care for our parents for years and years before they passed away. She's got a heart of gold. Still spoils me a bit, but I try to spoil her as well.'

Mike's head was spinning in confusion. He'd wanted Mary to be Kel's mother, not his *sister!*

'Sounds like you're a favourite,' he commented. He didn't trust himself to even say Mary's name, let alone reveal that he knew her. Instead, he found himself reverting back to the slightly safer subject of their shared appearance. Perhaps he could glean some more information that way. 'So, Kel,' Mike began, 'they say that everyone has a double, and here you are. I thought that my ugly dial was unique!' he laughed.

'I take exception to that! Not ugly … just "ruggedly masculine", as Katy says. I bet you had no trouble attracting the girls when you were younger!' Kel grinned. 'You probably could still if you wanted to, eh?' He gave Mike an exaggerated nudge.

'No, I'm over all that. I've only really loved one person, and that was my first girlfriend. Nobody else has even come close.'

'I hope you don't mind me asking,' Kel said, 'but earlier you said you were divorced. Was that the same girl?'

'No, someone else. My one marriage was a big mistake. You live and learn. Anyway, I don't want to drag down a good chin-wag, so let me get you some coffee.'

Eventually, with dinner and conversation drawing to an end, Kel glanced at his watch.

'Must go,' he said with a sigh. 'I drop in here now and then when Katy's on nightshift so I don't have to cook. Might see you if you're game enough to come here again!'

'I'll be here every night for the next week or so. I'll keep an eye open for your … um … rugged masculine features!' Mike taunted, as they both rose to leave.

The two men shook hands and exchanged business cards, even though Mike had just sold his landscaping business.

Kel's card read *Kelvin Williams, Financial Advisor*, with the usual contact details.

Mike was determined not to lose it. It might be useful.

***

Again at the restaurant, one scorching late afternoon, Mike was back on the deck, but this time he was sitting under the cover of a large white umbrella. He watched for any dive-bombing seagulls over unprotected tables, but no other diners suffered his previous fate. He hadn't seen Kel again since their evening a few nights ago, but still hoped he might drop in to Reflections, as his holiday was nearly over. Apart from having his own personal reasons, he really enjoyed the man's entertaining company.

Mike thought he would use Kel's business card to at least phone to say goodbye and thank the man for his help if he didn't turn up again. He had one more day up his sleeve before flying home.

Halfway through his meal, Mike noticed a baby gull pattering on the deck toward his table. With a few clumsy upward flaps, it perched on the back rail of the opposite chair, sitting there quietly with perfect manners. It just looked at Mike quizzically, allowing him to finish his meal.

In gratitude, Mike very slowly stretched out the palm of his hand, offering some morsels of bread to the young bird. It hopped onto the edge of the table to Mike's outstretched hand. It gently pecked and swallowed the crumbs, uttered a tiny squeak, fluttered down again, and disappeared below some wooden steps.

'Wasn't that the most precious thing?' asked a woman two tables away, fanning her face with the menu.

'Yes, pretty special,' Mike agreed. 'Not at all like normal seagull behaviour!' He looked carefully at the woman's beautiful smile.

'Excuse me, but is your name Mary Williams by any chance?' he asked, his heart thumping fast. 'Or maybe you've got a different surname now.'

'No, it's always been Williams,' she said.

'How do you know my name? Are you from Goulburn too?'

Mike gasped and removed his brimmed hat. He hurried over to Mary, lowering his voice so that the moment would be theirs alone.

'No, I'm from Melbourne. Mary, it's Mike. Mike Hargreaves. Don't you remember me?'

It was Mary's turn to gasp. She rose from her table and stood on tiptoe, flinging her arms around him. Mike bent down to reciprocate, adding a tender kiss. They settled at her table, holding hands, as they excitedly retraced their years apart.

Kel arrived to meet his sister but, after seeing the pair sitting at the table together, he detoured to a corner of the bistro, out of sight. He ordered drinks for Mary and Mike, asking the head waitress to pretend they were on the house.

Mike and Mary soon established that their enforced breakup had been a life-long deep regret.

'I tried to find you.' Mike explained. 'Do you know how many Williamses there are in Australia? I didn't know your Dad's initials, so I had no idea where to start.' His eyes searched Mary's intently. 'I'm pretty sure I know why your parents whisked you away. I knew there was a chance you might pregnant. Am I right? Were you having my baby?'

Mary nodded her head and wept quietly into

her lace handkerchief. Mike put a comforting arm around her. She found her voice again, relieved to finally unburden her painful secret to the one person she trusted. 'You should have been told. I *wanted* to tell you. I pleaded with my parents, but they banned me from contacting you. I didn't dare disobey – I was too scared and ashamed.' Mary wiped away more tears. 'They waited until they could see I was starting to fill out in the middle, and then Mum announced that *she* was having her eighth baby. She told everyone that the pregnancy had to be monitored by a city obstetrician. She'd stay in Sydney until the delivery, and I'd go with her, for company. We boarded in the city until *my* baby was born.'

Mike's heart raced. He wanted to show Mary the true compassion he felt for her, although, inwardly, he was elated about being a father. 'You poor darling,' he said. 'I'm just sorry I wasn't there for you.'

'That wasn't your fault. I knew you would've stuck by me,' she said confidently.

Mike nodded in agreement. 'So your baby brother was really your own baby – and my baby, too! His name's Kel, isn't it?'

Mary's mouth opened in astonishment.

'How do you know Kelvin? What's been going on?' Mary frantically looked around the restaurant. 'Did someone tell him I'm his mother? Tell me quickly – he's going to be here soon.'

'No, he doesn't know anything as far as I can tell,' Mike said softly, trying to calm Mary down. 'Nothing's going on. I just met Kel by chance, right here. He'd noticed our likeness and commented on it. During our chat, he showed me a photo that had you in it. I recognised you immediately, but didn't dare say a word about knowing you. I'd already put two and two together. He's a good bloke. You and your parents did a great job.'

Mary intently looked into Mike's eyes. He felt as though she was entering the very depths of his soul.

'Mike,' she finally spoke. 'I made a promise to my parents when Kelvin was born that he'll never know I am his birth mother. They went to a lot of trouble to keep my son in my life and I'll always be grateful for that. I've never married because I wanted to help take care of him until he grew up.'

'I'm so dreadfully sorry I wasn't there for you, but I did try. I think you're wonderful. Kel said you took care of your parents, too.'

'Yes, they were both unwell. It was the least I could do after all they did for me and our boy.'

'I promise I'll never mention it, sweetheart,' said Mike. 'He might work it out for himself one day, but he'll never hear it from me.'

With those words, their course was set. The couple linked arms as they reflected upon the unusual circumstances leading to their chance meeting. Reflections certainly was an apt name for the restaurant.

As darkness fell, Kel joined them at last, knowing his favourite sister would be wondering where he was. They had a wonderful time explaining how they'd all connected, greatly in awe of the role that seagulls had played in Mike and Mary's reunion!

A flock of noisy gulls circled above, then swooped across the water. Mike gave them the thumbs up.

'Thanks, chaps! You can all go home now. You've done a great job!'

Busybody

B eing a concerned citizen, but a pensioner of scant means, Shirley Carter wondered what she could do to help. The subject of domestic violence had been widely discussed across the various forms of media, so it was impossible to ignore. There had been a strong focus upon its terrible effects and its prevention. The statistics were alarming – almost unbelievable. It seemed that every week, more cases were being brought to the public's attention. And they were just the tip of the iceberg! Courageous survivors, their supporters, the police and politicians were joining forces to try to bring about positive change.

It soon became obvious to Shirley that victims could be living in her own area, as the problem was so widespread. In the light of that, she found that her antenna was working overtime. Did that make her a busybody? If she was, she hoped it was in a good way.

After thinking it through, Shirley decided that she'd merely do what she'd always done: continue to be on friendly terms with any people she knew from the surrounding streets. It was surprising how many she'd first met while weeding or watering her front garden. Occasionally, a passing 'hello' turned into a longer chat over a cuppa. The pleasant time together was usually spent in catching up with family news and the like, but occasionally someone just needed a sympathetic ear.

One of those people was Heather, a woman who'd appreciated Shirley's support when her second daughter, Chloe, became pregnant at sixteen. A baby boy was born who soon became his Grandma's delight, although, becoming a grandparent at thirty-eight hadn't sat well with Heather initially!

One grey cloudy day, Shirley was doing her usual spot of weeding when Heather stopped to say hello. It was her babysitting day, so she was taking little Jake, now ten months old, for a walk in his stroller. As usual, the women agreed on what a truly bonny baby he was, but their admiring remarks may have taken too long, as he started to get restless.

'I think Jake might like to stretch his legs.

A passing 'hello' turned into a longer chat.

Bring him inside, Heather. We can play on the living room carpet, while you just relax with a cuppa. What do you think?' Shirley asked.

'Oh, that'd be great, thanks,' Heather replied.

Shirley went ahead to hold open the front door for the pair. The young grandmother wheeled Jake along the bordered path, enjoying its flowering spring bulbs, until she reached the door.

Just as she stretched out her arms to navigate the step, the grey clouds parted and bright sunbeams shone through one of Heather's sheer sleeves. It was in that moment Shirley noticed three large, dark bruises on the woman's upper arm.

Now don't jump to conclusions, Shirl, she thought. But she wasn't about to ignore the signs, either.

'Goodness me, Heather! What have you been up to? Your arm looks dreadful!' Shirley exclaimed, taking a step towards her. 'Do you mind if I have a look at it?' Her nursing instincts kicked in.

'Oh, don't worry about that,' Heather replied, jolted into the realisation that the tell-tale marks were visible. She took two steps back, covering the arm with her opposite hand. 'I bruise easily,' she continued, striving for an unconcerned tone. 'I just slipped and fell against the side of the bath when I was mopping the wet floor.'

'That must have been a very nasty fall,' Shirley commented.

'Yes, but I just remembered we can't stay after all. Thanks for the offer, though. Next time, maybe.'

'Oh, okay,' Shirley said. 'Well, you take care, dear,' she added quietly, watching Heather steer the fretful baby back down the path with hardly a word of farewell.

It seemed that the bearer of bruises wouldn't be coming in for a cuppa today.

***

One afternoon, Shirley recognised Heather's daughter, Chloe, with her little boy, in the food court of the small shopping plaza. She asked the young mother if she could join them, to which Chloe agreed, with a welcoming smile. Baby Jake was sitting up in a highchair, happily squeezing a sandwich through his fingers, as his mother was finishing her coffee.

Their conversation centred on childcare and other safe topics until Shirley tentatively brought up the subject of Heather's welfare.

'Chloe,' she began, 'I'm concerned about your mum. I noticed some bad bruising on her arm recently, and I feel that she might need some help. I'm only raising the subject with you because she might be at risk. Have you seen her arm? Are you and your sister aware of a problem? I must say that your mum's explanation of what caused the bruises failed to convince me.'

Shirley informed Chloe of Heather's story about her fall in the bathroom.

Biting her lip, Chloe paused, deliberately taking a long time to wipe her son's face and fingers before returning him to the stroller.

'Shirley, it might seem bad,' she said, 'but there's really nothing to worry about. Honestly. Mum's perfectly safe. Nobody's hit her, if that's what you're getting at. Thanks for asking, though. I know you've been worried, but please don't talk about this to anyone. People could get the wrong idea.'

Shirley promised that she could be trusted. However, she still wasn't satisfied …

***

The following day, Shirley purposefully dropped in to a ladies' fashion boutique where Heather's other daughter, Julia, worked as a sales assistant. She was only two years older than Chloe, but looked older than her twenty years. Dressed in smart, conservative business clothes, Julia handled customers with polite confidence.

Shirley waited until she was free before

fronting up to the counter. Julia, quickly recognising her customer, greeted Shirley then lowered her voice.

'Shirley, I'm glad you're here. We need to talk. I'm guessing that's why you're here?' she asked.

Relieved that her unexpected visit wasn't met with resistance, Shirley smiled and nodded to clarify her intention.

Julia returned the smile, equally relieved to have the chance for a chat. 'Wait here while I ask my boss for a break,' she instructed.

After gaining permission from her manager, Julia left her post and beckoned for Shirley to follow her through a narrow stockroom. Although it was just a small boutique, the aisle was lined with scores of beautiful formal gowns, each protected by a cover of clear plastic.

At the far end of the stockroom was a small vacant office. Julia ushered Shirley to a chair and closed the door. She quickly seated herself opposite her guest, behind a small desk.

Suddenly, any semblance of confidence was gone. Her lower lip and slender, manicured fingers trembled. She seemed almost childlike, struggling to find the right words to say as the seconds ticked on. Shirley's heart went out to the girl, taking pity upon her by speaking first. She had to ease the tension somehow.

'Julia, I don't know you quite as well as your

sister, but please just try to think of me as a friend who's trying to help your mum. Did you speak to Chloe yesterday? Is that why you want to talk with me now?'

'Yes,' Julia whispered, nodding. 'Chloe panicked and called in to see me straight after you'd spoken with her. We live together now, so we talked about the problem again last night. We decided it's time to get some help for Mum and Dad. The whole business has been going on ever since they were first married. Chloe and I grew up thinking every family had something to hide, but you just didn't talk about it.'

'Good grief! It's a wonder your poor mother's still here to tell the tale!' exclaimed Shirley.

Julia's eyes widened with alarm. 'You're barking up the wrong tree, Shirley,' she said quickly. 'Your instincts are good, but there's more you need to know.' She paused for breath. 'What Chloe said about Mum yesterday is all true. Nobody's been hitting her. But the story Mum told you was a lie. Chloe said you didn't believe it, so that got us worried.'

Puzzled, Shirley remained silent and nodded in encouragement for Julia to continue.

'Most of the time, Mum and Dad have a fairly good marriage, but now and then Mum falls into a black hole of mood swings and angry outbursts.' Julia's anxious face became flushed. 'Dad's the one who has to bear the brunt of it all. *He's* the one who's suffered years of abuse at *Mum's* hands! But it's his damn pride that stops him from getting help. He'd be too humiliated to confess that he suffers injuries because his wife beats him up!'

With unfortunate timing, Julia's manager knocked loudly on the door, announcing break-time was over.

Flustered, Julia scrawled her address and phone number on a scrap of paper and passed it to Shirley. 'Do you think you could come around to our place sometime tonight after Jake's in bed?' she whispered. Shirley nodded. 'Just ring me on that number. And thanks, Shirley,' Julia added.

***

Shirley drove up to the sisters' unit right on seven forty-five. Julia and Chloe welcomed her into their tiny sitting room, where a variety of savoury morsels were laid out on a coffee table with drinks soon arriving to accompany them. Jake had settled down to sleep, allowing his mother time to gather her thoughts. Chloe explained the domestic arrangement to Shirley.

'After Jake was born, Mum and Dad wanted us to stay with them, but I couldn't have my baby exposed to her outbursts. So all three of us left home and it's worked out well. We get on each other's nerves sometimes – after all, we are sisters! But most of the time we like living together. Because of Julia's wages and the single mothers' benefit, we can share the rent. Mum didn't have that kind of support when she was pregnant at sixteen. She was lucky though, because Dad loved her and wanted to marry her, anyway.'

'Obviously, Mum and Dad still have big problems, but the arrangement's good for the rest of us,' Julia added. 'In the past, I wouldn't have thought that Chloe could be so well organised, but she is. She's a very good mother and keeps our little unit looking spick and span too. That's hard with a ten-month-old who's getting into everything.'

Chloe smiled, lapping up her big sister's praise, as she passed around the tasty savouries.

They all kept on nibbling, as Shirley directed the conversation to the reason for her visit. Explaining that she was a retired nurse, she first asked Chloe a question regarding the contraceptive pill:

'If your Mum had a teenage pregnancy, I would have thought she'd strongly advise you to go on the pill if there was any chance of that happening again. Did that not happen, Chloe?'

'No, Mum didn't believe in using it, and as far as I know, she still doesn't.'

'Alright. I think we might be onto something

here. Have either of you ever thought that your Mum's aggression might have something to do with her monthly cycle? Would you say these outbursts are occurring once a month?'

'Yes, or thereabouts,' Julia replied. 'We'd sometimes wondered if there was that connection, but the PMS blues that we get are nothing like what Mum goes through. We've always thought it was because she had some kind of mental illness, but Dad doesn't. He just thinks that Mum's bad temper is a cross he has to bear.'

The anxious girls waited expectantly, seated on the couch with arms linked for moral support. Shirley rose from her chair, sipped a glass of water, walked around the room for a while, and then sat down again.

'If you were to describe all of your Mum's behaviour during those bad times, what would you say?'

'She has horrible mood swings that come on suddenly, then she gets really angry and blames Dad for everything,' Chloe said. 'It's scary. She says nasty, abusive things to him that she'd never say at other times.'

'Yes,' Julia agreed. 'And Chloe and I have always said that the verbal abuse is probably just as damaging to Dad as the physical abuse, maybe even more so. But it breaks our hearts to see her pushing and hitting and punching him.

We've tried to intervene at times, but he always orders us to leave the room.'

'So why was your Mum so badly bruised when I saw her? Had your Dad finally hit back after all this time?'

'No, it wasn't anything like that,' Chloe answered. 'When we asked, Dad told us that he was simply restraining her because she was coming at him with such force, and we believe him. He'd never deliberately hurt her.'

Shirley felt great compassion toward the troubled family, but sensed a nervous fluttering, too. These were textbook symptoms. The words she was about to say could be life-changing.

'Now girls, I'm not a GP, but nursing has taught me a lot. I don't want to give you false hope, but I'm as certain as I can possibly be that your Mum has been suffering from a condition called PMDD. It's a really severe form of Pre Menstrual Syndrome. Sometimes sufferers become deeply depressed, or even suicidal. Then there are others who might become violent, like your mother. But the good news is that, with the right medication, including the pill, PMDD can be controlled very effectively.'

Julia slowly lowered her head, covering her face with her hands, and sobbed with relief. Chloe leaned over, gently rubbing her sister's shoulders, with her own face awash with tears. Shirley wiped away the tears from her own eyes and offered the girls some tissues.

'Thank you, Shirley. Thank you so much,' said Chloe, which Julia softly repeated. When they were ready, Shirley talked about a possible strategy.

'Now Julia, you told me earlier today that Chloe and you had already made the decision to get help for your parents. If I give you some printed material on the subject, would you be willing to approach your mother first? I think you'd be the best ones to win her over, and then all three of you could work on your Dad. I'll be available if you need backup, but I'm certain you'll do fine. How does that sound to you?'

'Sounds like a good plan,' said Chloe. 'I think Mum will be easier to convince than Dad though, as long as we get her on a good week.'

'But surely he'd be willing to talk to someone if he knew that your mother could be helped, wouldn't he, Chloe?' Shirley asked.

'Dad's way behind the times on these things. He thinks Mum's behaviour will never change,' the young woman said. 'To him, it's a family matter. Even now, he still swears us to secrecy.'

'So why are you and Julia disobeying him now and getting help after all this time?'

'Well, firstly, despite all his mixed-up reasoning, Dad doesn't deserve to wear the blame for Mum's bruises after all the abuse he's suffered for so long. We're grown up now. We love them both, and want to take care of them.'

'I can see that. They'll be proud of you for what you're about to do. And secondly?' inquired Shirley.

Julia took a deep breath, smiled, and visibly relaxed.

'Because a very nice busybody cared enough to follow up on her suspicions,' she said gratefully, as the two sisters rose from the couch to give the busybody a warm hug.

Changing Places

The sun's strong beams pierced the double glazing on my daughter's city apartment, highlighting her ruffled red hair. Frantically darting between bedroom and bathroom, Fiona tossed her husband's only piece of hand luggage onto the bed, and squashed his toiletries into the remaining spaces. She rebuked him with an angry curse for not packing his own items. She had already packed large cases for two adults and two children. That wasn't an easy task considering their trip to the USA was for six months. Packing his hand luggage was all that she'd asked him to do and time was running out.

Being a peace-loving man, Ross ignored her cursing and apologised. He quickly sent their young son, Jack, ahead to the elevator to hold the lift while he grabbed the case and caught up. They were headed for the underground car park to complete the packing of the car. The matching maroon suitcases had been chosen by my daughter and initialled in gold for easy recognition. They'd have to be carefully handled. No scratches allowed. It seemed like a futile goal!

In the bedroom, Fiona was still on the warpath. I was next in her line of fire.

'Mum, I hope you're going to do something about your house while we're away. This is your big chance to spruce it up,' she said, applying some lipstick. 'You've let it go since Dad died; the garden's so overgrown, and I have to fight my way to the front door! I'm telling you now, if we come back from America to find everything's still looking shabby, I'll call in the bulldozers to flatten the lot!'

My youngest grandchild, at six years of age, had been pretending to be asleep on my lap, sucking her thumb. I was used to Fiona's bluntness and chose to ignore the insults, but not bold little Trudy, who now opened her eyes.

'I like Nanna's house,' she said, sticking up for me. 'Don't get the bulldozers, Mummy. That's mean.'

'Mummy wouldn't really do it,' I quickly chimed in. 'She loves the house, but I guess it does need a coat of paint. I'll see what I can do about it.' Trudy seemed reassured as she snuggled back on my lap.

'I'll believe it when I see it,' Fiona mumbled.

I didn't respond, pretending not hear my daughter's comment. Her harsh words could be hurtful at times.

There were reasons for the neglect. I'm slowing down a bit, and I was hoping for an offer of help from the family, but it didn't come. They'd been terribly busy.

Fiona seemed more controlled now. She looked very stylish in her designer outfit, as she circled the bedroom, notepad in hand, checking her 'To Do' list. Opening her new leather shoulder bag, she searched inside. Trying to find the last item on her list, without success, her agitation returned.

'Passports. Passports. Oh, no! What's my stupid husband done with our stupid passports? I can't trust him to do anything right. They won't let us on the flight! I distinctly remember telling him to put them in this bag.'

Ross is certainly *not* stupid. He and Jack returned just in time for Fiona's tirade. Ross was sure he'd put the passports in the shoulder bag.

Panicking, Fiona raced around from perfect room to perfect room, fossicking in drawers and banging doors. Ross, Jack, Trudy and I tried to help, but all we got was a tongue-lashing.

Five minutes passed. Ten minutes. We should've been leaving for the airport. Then Ross yelled from the bedroom.

'Got 'em!' he called.

We all ran in to see him holding up the shoulder bag.

'What's this?' he asked, pulling out the passport wallet with a flourish and a smirk.

Fiona rushed over to peer inside.

'Well, how was I to know there was another pocket right down there?' she snapped.

I wanted to laugh, but held it in. Fiona threw up her hands, swore again, apologised and grabbed her troublesome bag, as we all headed for the door.

'And you wonder why we've never been on a family holiday,' she muttered to me, with the hint of a smile.

The drive to the airport was subdued. I was mostly thinking about Fiona. I'd always been proud of her achievements in the financial world. She'd worked hard to get to management level, but I constantly worried about their pressured family life, and wondered if the marriage would survive. I was the one who took the children to their various activities every day after school. Ross usually cooked dinner, supervised Jack's homework, helped Trudy get ready for bed and listened to her reading. Fiona's schedule kept her away from home until 7:30 at least, so they'd all be tired and grumpy by then. On weekends they'd catch up with odd jobs, housework and homework to be organised for the following week. There wasn't much time left for play.

As we chatted in the airport's departure lounge, Jack borrowed Ross's phone to show me a map of the US, while Trudy peered around his shoulder.

'We're going to stay in Houston, Texas for the first couple of weeks,' he said, pointing to the right spot. 'They've got a humungous airport there and Mum says there's a lot to do around Houston. Then later we're going to a cowboy ranch near Dallas.'

'And when you've all had a good rest, you're going over to the east coast. That's right, isn't it?' I asked. 'Can you show me Washington DC and New York City on the map? It's Trudy's turn this time.'

Jack passed the phone over to his sister, who found the cities with hardly any help.

They were well prepared for where they were going – which was a credit to their parents.

'And on our way home we're going to Disneyland an' Hollywood!' she said excitedly, as Jack showed her where they were on the phone.

I looked over at Fiona and smiled. 'I'm glad you're extending your holiday, darling,' I said. 'The children will always remember it. Ross tells me he can't wait to get on the plane. This could be the happiest six months you've ever known'.

She gave a big sigh. 'I certainly hope so, Mum,' she said.

The family was in desperate need of quiet, unhurried time together – time to get to know each other again. If they couldn't find enjoyment in each other's company, I could only see heartbreak ahead.

Rummaging in her shoulder bag, Fiona pulled out her ever-present notepad to read through my list of instructions.

'You'll need to cancel the ladies' gym, and call my hairdresser and manicurist. My personal trainer knows about the trip, of course. I haven't had time to call the children's tennis coach, either. Their dance classes are finished, but you'll need to remind the swimming and karate instructors. The numbers are all written here.' She held the book up close to my nose. 'Are you sure you can read my writing?' she asked anxiously.

'Yes, it's fine,' I said, then added mischievously, 'Any cancellations for Ross?' I knew that he never had any time for his own pursuits. I wasn't very subtle and I knew it. Fiona ripped out my page and silently handed it to me.

I deliberately hadn't offered my services as a travelling childminder. Even though I was going to miss them greatly, I knew it was time to step back. I wondered how they'd go without my support. They had to learn. It was sink or swim. They'd never spent six days alone as a family unit, let alone six months! My anxious thoughts were interrupted by the boarding call.

I was surprised to feel that Fiona's cheeks were damp as we hugged goodbye. She was probably sharing my anxiety.

'You need a break, too, Mum,' she said kindly. 'Don't worry about getting the house painted. You could take up lace making again, or load up the car with your easel and paints, like you used to. Learn Spanish dancing or something. This is your chance to do something new, too. Just surprise us.'

'Be careful!' I cautioned her with a laugh. 'It might be more like a shock than a surprise! Thanks, darling,' I said more soberly. 'Love you. I'll miss you heaps.' I tried for a cheery smile, but didn't succeed.

A tight hug for each one and then they were on their own.

So was I.

It felt really strange – even a little scary!

***

I wouldn't have thought that five months and twenty-seven days could pass so quickly. I had thirty-one postcards on my fridge door; the latest showing that the little family was heading for home again. I could hardly contain my excitement at the prospect of their return.

At the airport, I found seats where I could wait right under the huge 'International Arrivals' sign. After a long delay, my gorgeous grandchildren were hugging me tight, with Fiona and Ross joining in. They seemed relaxed, happy and healthy, although obviously tired from the long trip.

'Can we all go to Nanna's please, Mum?' asked Jack, echoed by Trudy, with not a trace of whining.

It was late in the day, and here I was thinking they'd want to go straight home to recover.

'I hope so,' smiled Fiona. 'We've got heaps to tell you, Mum.'

Everyone in the car gasped as I drove up to my home with its new modern façade.

'Easily done,' I boasted brightly. 'Just a few longer windows, a bit of render, and some new landscaping in the garden.'

'Wow!' exclaimed Ross and the children from the backseat.

'That's amazing!' Fiona said, with eyes wide open.

We got out of the car and I enthusiastically ushered them through the vermillion front door to the updated interior of my home. They could see light, bright walls, antiqued floorboards, modern rugs, recessed shelving, and a stunning, up-to-date kitchen.

All of the accumulated clutter from the

last thirty-eight years had disappeared. What pleased me most were groups of my paintings lining some of the walls. Simple compositions, with strong colours; the oil paint was still tacky from my last minute touches. I'd never tried abstracts before so I was excited when they turned out as well as I'd hoped. The decorating style was very much Ross and Fiona's. I'd hoped they might like the changes.

Trudy and Jack just stared, perhaps confused by the lack of familiarity. Then they dropped onto a shaggy rug, tugged at the long tufts, and rolled around, annoying each other. Fiona's eyes darted around the main room, taking in the simple, sleek furniture.

'Those timber pieces go beautifully with the couches, Mum,' she said, voicing her approval. These positive comments continued as we moved around from room to room.

As a builder's contractor, nothing missed Ross's gaze. 'Your house really lends itself to this kind of update, Mum. It's still solid as a rock, but the plain rooms make a great backdrop for modern furnishings. You haven't had to pull down walls, or change anything structural. In fact, it's a very clever little renovation. Well done, Mum. Ten out of ten!' he said. My cheeks grew warmer as I lapped up his praise.

'I had a few headaches in the early stages,' I explained, 'but the renovators helped me work through them, and I learnt as we went along. Once the kitchen went in, one idea led to another, and I just got carried away. I thought tradesmen were meant to be difficult, but mine were wonderful. I just made sure there was plenty of my peppermint slice at coffee time!'

'You wouldn't know it was the same house as before, would you, Ross?' Fiona said, smiling at him.

I sensed some ambiguity in her words and guessed what she may have been thinking: the improvements were remarkable, but the atmosphere of the old family home was gone. I felt a twinge of guilt for not preparing her in advance for these changes.

Fiona stifled a yawn and her tired eyes brightened. She wanted to give me some news, too.

My thoughts darted wildly. I'd noticed that her slim figure was a little curvier than when they'd left for Houston. I'd initially put it down to those big servings of food at American restaurants. But could she be pregnant again? If that were the case, I wanted to be happy for them, but how would they cope? She'd only taken short breaks from work when Jack and Trudy were born, so they'd need my help more than ever.

Ross put an arm around her shoulder. They both smiled, excited about her announcement.

'I've decided to leave the company, Mum. Trying to do everything is just too hard to juggle. I didn't realise how much my absences were affecting everyone at home, or how much of a load you and Ross were carrying. It's just not worth all the stress.'

'And I'm sick of the builders I work for,' chimed in Ross, 'so we're going to set up some sort of business to run from home. Maybe it'll be related to building or finance; maybe something totally different.'

I was speechless for a few seconds then warmly hugged them both.

'Oh, you don't know how pleased I am!' I exclaimed. 'That's wonderful news! And whatever you choose to do, you'll do well. I've got great confidence in both your abilities.'

Their happy faces and a sigh from Fiona, told me they were relieved to have my support.

'We want to sell our city apartment ASAP,' Ross continued, 'and look for something not too far from you. While we were away we had plenty of time to talk about priorities. We want to bring up the kids in some peace and quiet. Maybe we could buy one of those country homesteads down the highway.'

Ross offered to put the kettle on, but I, surprising them, declined his offer.

I stood up and mysteriously beckoned them all to follow me out of the front door, locking it behind us. I'd thought hard about how to manage this next surprise, and had decided this was the best way. They continued to follow me out through the gate and along the footpath, until we stopped five houses away from mine.

'Welcome to my new home!' I announced, marching them up the winding path to a lovely, two-year-old clinker brick cottage.

***

Once I'd opened the front door, the children burst inside, excited footsteps muffled by the cosy carpet, as they raced through the house, pointing out the familiar furnishings: the loaded bookshelves, the big cushioned couch, the old dining table, the family photos and some treasured ornaments.

Fiona walked around the living area, with hands clasped under her chin, like a child in prayer. Ross joined her, standing close, as she reminded him of the reason each object held precious memories for her.

'Mum, this place is beautiful,' she said, wiping away a tear. 'It's got the feel of the old house as it used to be.'

The children grabbed Ross by each hand and began to drag him toward the other rooms.

'Can I have a look at the rest of the house, Mum?' he called over his shoulder, disappearing down a short hallway. Jack and Trudy soon returned to do the same for their mother.

'Okay, you two,' she laughed. 'I think I can find my own way. Why don't you stay here and tell Nanna all about the cowboy ranch in Texas?'

My grandchildren did just that, while their parents explored my new abode.

As I listened to their great adventures – including their time in Disneyland and Hollywood – I filled the kettle, toasted some thick bread and smeared it with Vegemite for them. They were so grateful, they even said 'Thank you' without being reminded. They happily ate it all, sprawled on the couch, watching television.

Ross and Fiona finished their tour in the kitchen.

'It's a ten out of ten for this place, too, Mum,' Ross said, giving me a thumbs up. 'And I think you've been hiding a talent for interior decorating. The styles of both houses are very different, but the presentation in each one is stunning.' Fiona enthusiastically agreed with him.

I thanked Ross for his comments, feeling my cheeks warming with pleasure, once again.

'Don't even think about cooking a meal, Mum,' Fiona added, as I opened the pantry door. 'Toast'll do for us too. I'll do it. You just relax.'

My daughter usually avoided kitchens, so I happily accepted, privately pleased. Soon, the three of us were at the table, hands wrapped around mugs of hot tea, enjoying grilled cheese on toast, and chatting about their wonderful holiday.

Fiona looked across at me with a smile. 'I know you'll have to sell the old house now, Mum, but I won't mind. Honestly. This place feels like home already.'

The children seemed at home too, already sound asleep on the couch.

'I have to tell you something,' I confessed. 'The old house is already on the private market. The agent was getting a few enquiries and I need to sell. There's one written offer, but there won't be a sale unless they come up to my price. I want to know your thoughts too, Ross, and hopefully, have your blessing.'

'You've got it,' he said quickly. 'You've made some very wise decisions, with no input from us. You're a property developer now!'

Fiona's weary eyes suddenly widened.

'That's it!' she yelled. 'Property development could be our new business! You could take care of the creative side, Mum. Ross could handle all the renovations, and I could manage the projects and finances. We'd make a good team.'

Coughing and spluttering while trying to sip my tea, I recoiled at the idea of coming out of retirement. I'd left the working world years ago, although I had to admit that the idea had merit. It would call upon our individual abilities.

Ross sat silently thinking for what seemed ages. Finally he spoke.

'Okay … It's not a bad idea at all. If we all agree, Fiona could run through some rough figures to see if we could make a go of it. If they look promising, I'll be in it. If we only take on small projects, buy wisely, and stick to our own fields of expertise, it should work. That way, Fiona and I would still be able to give the kids the time and attention they deserve and, hopefully, still be speaking to each other at the end of the day!' he added with a wink.

It was now my turn to say something.

'Sorry, Ross,' I said, 'but I don't think you need to include me in the arrangement. I think the business should simply be a husband-wife partnership, with me on the sidelines, lending a creative hand as it's needed. I'd probably be quite busy at the start and end of each project, but that would be enough to keep me out of mischief. Anyway, sorting that out can wait. It's getting late. Let's get everyone back into their own beds, so we can sleep on the idea. My goodness, what a day it's been!'

***

There was no sleeping in. Early the next morning, I was awoken by the bedside phone's low buzz. Slowly, I sat upright, swung my feet down to the carpet, pulled the floral doona around my shoulders and reached for the phone. It had to be Fiona. My friends, sensibly, leave me alone till I've had my coffee.

'Hello, darling,' I mumbled huskily. 'Give me five minutes. I'll ring you back.'

'No, wait a minute, Mum,' she said. 'This is about the old house. You need to talk to your agent straight away.'

With the phone tucked under my chin, I snuggled back into bed, suddenly remembering the previous night's discussion. Her words tumbled out rapidly, despite the early hour. Perhaps she'd never heard of jetlag!

'Mum, could you put a hold on the sale of the house? *Please.* We'd like to buy it ourselves, especially if we're going to be working together at times. Maybe the country homestead idea wasn't quite our style; but our apartment furniture would look amazing with your renovation. And Trudy and Jack could visit you anytime. It's just the perfect arrangement. Oh! And I've already crunched some numbers, and we're sure we could have a sound little business up and running in no time.'

'Whoa! Hold on. I need to wake up first. Thanks, darling. I'll get back to you as soon as

I can. Bye.' I hung up the phone. My head was spinning. I needed that coffee. I was happy to be involved to a lesser degree with the business idea, and I knew that Ross and Fiona could easily afford the asking price for my house. But something else felt not quite right.

It was that little sentence: *Trudy and Jack could visit you anytime.* I realised why I was uneasy. As much as I absolutely adore my grandchildren, I just wasn't prepared anymore to be a seven-days-a-week, 'on call' childminder without a life of my own. I wanted to be able to write an engagement in my diary, and not have to pull out at the last minute because there was nobody available to go on a school excursion or pick them up from karate or take them to the dentist, or a birthday party. Once I had to go to parent-teacher interviews, for goodness' sake!

I'd changed since then. Certainly, Fiona had changed too. And being home-based should help her to be available after school hours. The problem as I saw it was that her enthusiasm for the new business might cause her to fall back into old habits, especially if I was so handy.

Living five doors away was *not* going to work out!

***

Ten minutes of walking the floor and sipping hot coffee did the trick. Panicking, I rang the estate agent.

'Paul, about that written offer. I've got good news. I'm willing to come all the way down to the buyer's price, as long as I have a sale immediately. It's urgent. Something's come up. Ring me back as soon as you've spoken to him, please.'

Five minutes later, the agent called me back with the news I wanted to hear. My house officially had a buyer.

'Thank you so much, Paul. You're a treasure. Before you go, I have to confess something. I'm going to tell my daughter that you spoke to the buyer late last night, and that you clinched the deal then.'

'Um, okay,' Paul said. I sensed uncertainty in his voice.

'It will get me out of a tight spot with my family,' I explained. 'They'll assume *he* came up to *my* price. I'll fill you in when I come in to sign the papers.'

'No worries,' he replied, still sounding somewhat unsure. 'Is there anything else I can do for you?'

I thought fast.

'Perhaps there is,' I replied. 'Tell me, is that gorgeous architect-designed house near the vineyards still for sale? You know the one – it's about five kilometres down the highway from here.'

'The contemporary one with lots of weathered metal and timber?'

'That's the one,' I said, trying not to sound too excited.

'Yes, it's still for sale.'

'Great!' I said and tried to regain my composure. 'Would you say it's a spacious home?'

'Well, for a start it's got five bedrooms,' he replied. 'And a nice family room with an adjoining smart kitchen.'

'And would there be space for a home office too?' I asked hopefully.

'There's a sizeable office there already,' Paul confirmed. 'Not only that – there's an impressive storage shed as well.'

'Fantastic!' I felt more confident than ever now. 'I think I've got the perfect buyers for it, but I'll need to do some fast talking. Just leave it to me. Thank you so much. I'll let you know how I get on.'

After that very successful phone call, my excitement soon gave way to a classic case of nerves. My heart raced, palms were sweaty and my stomach churned.

Twice, I reached for the phone to ring Fiona but decided that crumpets and another mug of coffee were more important. What if they saw through my deception and the reason for it, too? Could I trust Paul to keep my secret about the deal? I wasn't comfortable with what I'd done. Another half hour passed by. Enough of this delay!

Just as I moved toward the phone, it rang. It was Ross.

'Mum, I've got Fiona with me here, and we've got some disappointing news for you. I'm afraid we won't be able to buy your house after all. Space is going to be a problem. We're sorry to let you down. I'll hand you over to Fiona to explain, but I should warn you that she's a bit anxious and teary at the moment.'

'Everything's going to be fine,' I said, reassuringly. 'Firstly, don't give the old house a second thought. The agent just told me he's sold it! I only found out this morning.'

There was no need for me to be devious, either! A pity about the lower price, though.

Between sniffles, and confusing comments, it took me a few seconds to catch on to what Fiona was now saying.

'I don't know what happened, Mum. We were being careful. But I've done a quick test, and it seems that there's another baby on the way! And then there's setting up the new business, and selling the apartment, and checking out schools, and moving goodness knows where? How can I manage morning sickness and aching backs and everything else? But I'm happy about the baby. I really am.'

'Oh! Oh! What a beautiful surprise! It's wonderful news. Dry your tears – you won't have to do it all alone.' I heard a big sigh from the other end of the line, followed by a little 'thanks Mum'.

'Ross is a bit shocked, but pleased,' Fiona continued. 'He even joked about having a fourth one for a playmate; at least, I *think* he was joking!'

'Let's get Baby Number Three into the world first,' I suggested. We both laughed. 'But more importantly,' I added, 'this is going to be a wonderful time for all of you. You and Ross are capable of being great parents *and* marriage partners *and* business partners if you'll allow yourselves the time to enjoy it all. You won't need me as a childminder quite as often once life settles down a bit. I'm your children's Nanna, not their employed nanny. There's a difference between the two ... but only *you* can be their Mummy.'

There was a long pause. Had I said too much? I could hear her blow her nose.

'Okay, Mum. I hear you loud and clear. But you're *my* Mum, and I'm going to need your help to get everything organised. Will you be there for me?'

'Of course, darling. Oh! And I just had a thought: would you and Ross be interested in having a look at a gorgeous contemporary house down the highway? It's all chunky timber and glass and weathered metal, with enough room for more babies and lots of family space. There's even a big office area for a home-based business. It's got your names written all over it!'

About the Author

Baby boomer Ruth Philbrick lives in Melbourne with her husband Robin, four family pets and the occasional wandering echidna.

Upon leaving school, she was employed as a showcard artist in major department stores. After marrying and becoming a mother of three, she freelanced on various art projects.

In 1993, Ruth took up oil painting and composition of verse, as well as dabbling in short story writing as relaxation after the onset of cancer.

This collection is a celebration of good health, after another more recent remission from cancer. As Ruth approaches seventy, her love of family, friends, church and community is stronger than ever.

Discussion Questions

Never Too Late.

This story's title certainly applies to Susan and Tom. In real life, is it always so? Does another saying, 'Seize the day' ('carpe diem') relate to 'Never Too Late'?

Ray of Sunshine.

Not everyone has Ray's special talents. Not every nursing home resident has the capacity to socialise. But, generally speaking, what can we learn from her if we also need nursing home care?

The Pianola.

What do you think were Kevin's thoughts when Andy asked about regularly opening his home to the troubled boys? What might have been his pros and cons?

Service with a Smile.

Polly had been volunteering her time and efforts for many, many years. Although this reveals a giving heart, is there anything in the story to suggest that she also receives?

Too Good to be True?

What was your reaction to Carolyn's carefree abandonment of her niggling doubts? Do your thoughts reflect how you view yourself, as a true romantic, someone who likes to be more considered in matters of the heart, or a bit of each?

Magazine Man.

In your opinion, why did the old man have such an impact on the young narrator?

Testing Times.

Mr. Woods seems to be a flawless example of his profession. Did his resolution of Ellie and her mother's problem disappoint or please you?

It Started in the Sixties.

What was your response to the inclusion of that one small word? A yawn? Amusement? A pleasing surprise? Unsettling disapproval? Did your reaction reflect your own beliefs on a subject that can still be polarising?

Labours of Love.

Do you think that Kerrie should have told Trish about the recipients of her baby clothes? Was it important to know, or not? (Think about the eventual result of sharing that information.)

Reflections.

Did you wonder about the outcome of Mike and Mary's rekindled love? Do you think it probable that Kel would guess his birth parentage, sooner or later? What would you predict his reaction could be?

Busybody.

Have you ever suspected that someone you know is suffering abuse from their partner or a parent? (Either physically, verbally, or both.) Would you have the courage to try to help in some way?

Changing Places.

Is there a possibility that Fiona might have, initially, been trying to keep her mother occupied, following the death of her father? Or that Fiona and Ross wanted to include her in their new business for the same reason? Is there any evidence for this?

Notes

Notes

Notes

Notes

Notes

Notes